# Hero of the Fallen

W. Sherry

2nd Edition



ISBN:
ISBN-13: 9781690002710

To:
Sarah, Sawyer, & Boone

Thanks to:
Mo & Mossy M.
Amy C.
Emily R. M.
Brandon A.

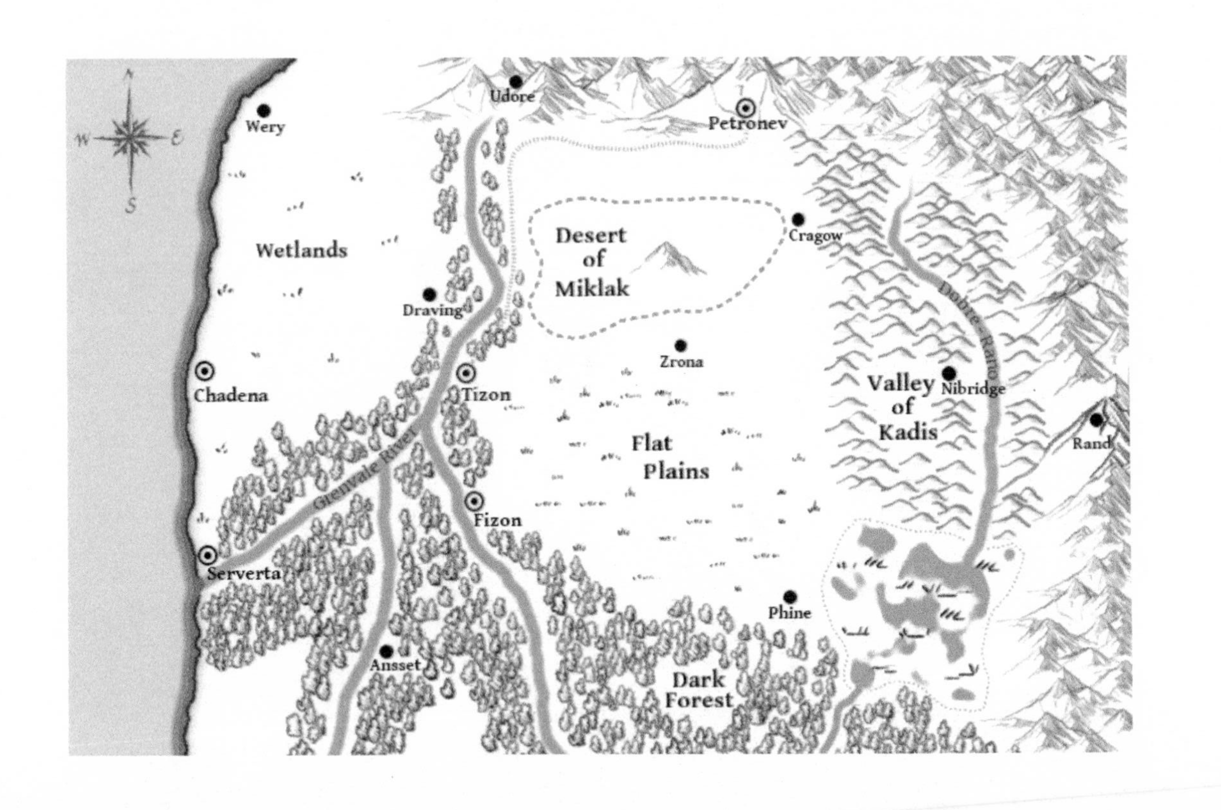
N
W
E
S
Wery
Udore
Petronev
Wetlands
Desert
of
Miklak
Cragow
Draving
Zrona
Chadena
Tizon
Valley
of
Kadis
Nibridge
Dobre - Rano
Rand
Glenvale River
Flat
Plains
Fizon
Serverta
Phine
Ansset
Dark
Forest

# 1

Will stirred, blinking his eyes as the room began to come into focus. *Tonight is the night.* Will had always had a constant desire that he struggled to communicate to others, namely when he did something dangerous. It was a wild desire that made him want to fight with other boys, play war, and throw rocks at anything within range. Lately, though, he felt as if this deep burning had been locked in a cage striving to get out. Will felt the knot inside him holding the cage shut when he swallowed. If he had to keep it shut up much longer, he felt he would surely die. *Oh, to be free!* Will had always longed for freedom, though he saw it as a wish he would never see fulfilled. No one had ever left the village. But tonight was the night when the beast within him would finally be set free. Tonight he felt he might truly live.

The village of Rand sat halfway up the Mount of Fallow. Rand was built on the ruins of an ancient city, which must have been great, judging by the remaining architecture. Plundering and burning had destroyed what it once had been. Massive stone walls and building foundations had been taken over by crawling vegetation. Within Rand, there were many amateur archeologists between the ages of six and sixteen. The underground tunnels, caverns, and ruins were their favorite places to play. What was peculiar about this village, though, is that once the children turned sixteen, they no longer desired to explore the old city.

When younger children played and ran over the remaining stone structures, adults would stare longingly into nothingness for a moment and then admonish them, "You have fun while you can, kids."

When asked the question all children ask—why?—the adults only shook their heads and said, "You'll understand why when you're older." The adults wore a sense of loss on their faces as they spoke these words.

After a few deep breaths and a stretch, Will's eyes fixated on the various patterns in the thatched ceiling. He laid on his straw bed in the quaint two-room hut built by his father, and he pondered his life. Like most fifteen-year-old boys, he pondered what his purpose was, the reason for his existence, and those things which intrigued him most. Will relished thinking deeply and discussing his complex thoughts with others. He was taller than other boys his age, which meant he stood eye to eye with most men in the village, his father being one of the exceptions. Will was wiry and strong. He had black hair and brown eyes. He often had a stubbly beard that he shaved in order to avoid revealing the bare spots. The thing that set him so far apart from other fifteen-year-olds was not his thoughts or his looks, but it was his passion.

As Will laid there, his younger brother Peran drooled beside him, saliva soaking into his crow-feather stuffed pillow. Peran breathed the deep, steady breaths of one who was actually asleep, not faking. His breaths seemed to lull Will into grogginess. They reminded him of his life: mundane, repetitive, and boring. But today Will hoped for change. Today he turned sixteen. Today he truly became a man in his village. Emanating from the core of his being and spreading to the tips of his fingers and toes, excitement coursed through his veins.

As he thought about his upcoming birthday celebration that night, his heart surged. He felt the steady drip of adrenaline into his system, and he opened his eyes wide. Will wanted adventure and freedom, like the stories of heroes that his dad, Merle, would sometimes tell him and his brother around the fire.

The day passed slower than most as Will did the regular chores: sweeping the floors of the hut, fetching water from the well, helping his brother, etc. Every once in a while, he caught glimpses of his father out in the village talking with other men. This was strange because his father always said, "Son, daylight is for working. If you aren't working in the light you might as well be blight."

Dad was almost always in the large forge that took up nearly half of the village. All men who were not too old worked there, making weapons to trade with the merchants who came to the village every month.

* * *

As the sun set and Will's family gathered for dinner, there was not a single mention of Will's birthday. It almost seemed as if the entire family had forgotten, even his mother. Will felt as if he had been punched in the gut. All the excitement that had built up inside him began to deflate. He drooped his head, until it almost touched the table. His arms felt like noodles, and his blood drained from his face. His heart rate began to slow. *Boom...boom....* Confused, he snapped back into reality.

"Wha— what?" he said, now noticing his father addressing him.

"What has got you all sour, boy?"

Always honest with his father, he said, "You forgot my birthday, Pop."

"Did I?" Will's father picked up a small deerskin drum from beside the table.

*Where did that come from?*

He began a steady beat. It grew louder but not from within the hut. There were others outside.

*Boom, dum...boom, dum...boom, dum.* Will's heart began to race again. The drums breathed life into what had been a disheartened spirit.

Once Will was fully resuscitated, his father pulled on his deerskin coat. He told Will to leave his shirt behind. All Will would need was his trousers.

*That's a strange request.* Will thought it, but he did not say it. He obeyed his father.

His father opened the door into the brisk, dark night.

When Will stepped out, he saw stars beyond count. The only thing that hindered the lights in the sky was a small, smoky fire surrounded by men, which burned in the center of the village. Almost all forty of the mountain village men aged sixteen and older were there.

Will's father guided him toward a spot directly in front of the fire. "Kneel."

Will put one knee on the ground, bracing himself on the other. His father grabbed something out of a jar and threw it on the fire. *Crack!* The fire seemed to break. It grew from a small campfire into a raging furnace, simultaneously illuminating the faces and bodies of all those standing around it. The expressions worn by the men were not ones of happiness or joy, but of somber reality. It made Will feel slightly queasy. That is, until he saw his father showing white teeth in a beaming smile.

The drumming stopped, but Will's heart beat the rhythm of the drums that no longer sounded. *Boom, dum... boom, dum... boom, dum.* He knelt, awestruck. *What is this?* The fire danced in his eyes.

"Son."

He looked to his father. "Yes, sir?" he replied, unsure of the proper way to address his father in this context.

"Look at the sky. What do you see?"

*What was happening? The sky, darkness, bright stars, a few clouds. What was the right answer?* "I only see the darkness and the stars, Father."

"Look at the ground and tell me what you see."

Will looked down. It was the normal ground he had seen his whole life, nothing special. He looked harder. *Green grass, gray rock, moss on the rock... What am I supposed to be seeing?* At a loss, with all eyes staring at him, he replied, "I only see what has always been there, grass and rock."

"Remember what you have seen. It is now time for

you to know our history and our bane, Will. Have you ever wondered why our people never leave the mountain? Have you ever wondered why we work as blacksmiths? Do you ever wonder where we ship our goods to?"

*I have often wondered.* Anytime he'd asked, Will had always been told, "You will know when you become older."

His father went on. "Two hundred forty-one years ago, there was a great war. It was the war to end all other wars. Every man was called to arms. Farmer or noble, all were called, and all fought. We do not know much of our people's roles, other than our ability to craft metal. We presume we are a special class of smiths, due to our ability to make specialized weaponry. What we do know is this: we stood by the old king and our side lost. As a result, our people were banished to this mountain and forced to work for the emperor."

"The emperor?" Will questioned. *Who? What? We don't have a ruler. Do we?*

"Our work goes to the empire, and they do with it as they please. Once we tried to refuse them our blacksmithing. They came in and murdered our chief's children. The emperor then brought his magic workers to confine us to this mountain. The magic keeps us here. It is why we are unable to leave."

"Why are we so despised, Father?"

"We can only guess, but we do know one thing. Our people are special."

At this point, the village chief, Boxfen, brandishing a knife, approached Will. Will looked to his father with fear. Chief Boxfen and Will's father both knelt. Will's eyes were trained on the knife. The chief gave a yank on the singular knife. It came apart into two pieces—identical, mirror images of one another. He handed one to Will's father.

Will's father whispered to his son, "Be brave, and no matter what, you fight for what is right."

Father's rough and calloused hands forced Will to bend at the abdomen so that his back was exposed. He and Chief Boxfen rested the points of the knives next to Will's spine—one on the right side, the other on the left.

Will felt the coldness of steel poking into his skin just above his shoulder blades. As the chief began to chant in some ancient tongue, that thing inside Will that had bothered him for years started to shake in its cage. Will didn't know which was stronger, fear or anticipation. The chief abruptly stopped, and Will took a deep breath in anticipation of whatever would happen next. All of a sudden, he saw a bright light. And then darkness.

# 2

"Will. Will. *Will!* Wake up!" His father's voice sounded as it always did, strong and confident.

Will felt pain across his back above his shoulder blades where the ceremonial knives had slit his skin. He opened his eyes. The fire seemed brighter than usual. Repelling the assault on his fuzzy vision, Will turned face down. The ground no longer looked as it had before. It was not just green with gray rocks. A dust-like substance of blue and purple covered it. He thrust his head upward, hoping to shake off whatever had happened. Purple haze, like curtains, had been drawn around the mountain that he had always called home. What had happened to him?

"Will, it is alright."

Will turned toward the voice, but the man who said his name no longer looked like his father. He was the same size and shape and had the same trimmed beard, but this man was covered in blue symbols. His eyes were no longer brown; they were blue. His face bore what looked like a blue tattoo. A thick, blue V marked his forehead. Below his eyes were two diagonally slanting lines. Will turned, confused, and looked around. All the men had the same bright-blue tattoos on their faces, and they all had crystal-blue eyes. Continuing to scan his surroundings, he noticed that the entire gathering bore purple-tattooed shackles on their wrists and ankles.

Someone, Will couldn't say who, brought him a bowl of water to see his reflection. Will looked like the rest of the village, burning-blue eyes, the blue V tattoo on his forehead, and two diagonal slants under his eyes. *What am I? What are we?* He looked around for the answer, not realizing he hadn't spoken audibly.

"Merle." The chief sounded pensive as he addressed Will's father in a hushed tone. "Your son has no shackles."

All eyes locked onto Will. He heard someone whisper, "The curse must be weakening."

Will's father did not acknowledge the comment, but asked Will to stand.

Will, weak from blood loss, felt light-headed at first but quickly recovered. He began to put together the events and remembered that his back had been ripped open from his spine to his shoulder by knives.

When Will's feet were firmly on the ground and his head cleared, his father addressed him.

"Will, you are now a man in the eyes of this tribe, and in the eyes of the king, if he exists."

"If he exists," the men repeated in unison.

The air felt colder in Will's lungs, but that was not all. Something had changed within him. The caged thing inside him—that passion, that desire for adventure—no longer ached. It was no longer caged.

Instead, Will's passion flowed through him. As though he was made for something great, Will felt excitement with every breath. *What was just released inside of me? What does this mean?*

The whole process left him with many questions, but what he didn't question was that he was a man. He kept repeating to himself, *Be brave. Fight for what's right.*

Will's father spoke, addressing the crowd. "Thank you all for coming to my eldest son's entrance into manhood. He is now deserving of honor and respect."

The men shifted, trying to get closer.

"They want to see a son of the village without shackles." Will's father explained. "No one living or dead, from what we know, has ever beheld such a sight," He and Chief Boxfen pushed through the crowd and guided Will back to his home.

Will still didn't understand why they all had shackles. From the youngest man present to the oldest, they all bore the fetters of captivity. *Where are my shackles?* "Pop, I have so many questions."

"There will be a time for your questions later. For now, you need to rest, and we will talk in the morning." His father was obviously bothered.

Once home and in his bedroom, Will collapsed in exhaustion. The last thing he could make out before falling asleep was the chief and his father earnestly discussing something in hushed voices.

"Will, get up! We don't have much time. Say goodbye to your mother and brother."

Will opened his eyes, immediately alert. It was still dark. "Wha—what is it, Pop?"

"We must leave right now." His father's eyes were still blue and still had the tattoo around them.

*It was real. It was not a dream.*

Will's mother was crying. "I love you, Will!" She heaved between sobs and then, looking him intently in the eyes, her own eyes blue as well, she said, "Find the truth, Will." She embraced him in a hug and gave a sloppy wet kiss.

"What's going on? I'm not going anywhere," Will said indignantly.

"Will, we must leave now. Do not argue with me. I will explain on the way." Will's father spoke with the utmost sternness.

Will thought about resisting his father's command, but he had never had reason to doubt him. Patting Peran on the head as he slept, Will whispered, "Goodbye, brother. I love you."

Emotion started to overtake him, and tears trickled down his cheeks. *Whatever adventure I am on, I don't want it. I want my family.*

Will's father gave him a minute to gather his composure. Then they hoisted their prepacked sacks onto their shoulders and went into the dark night.

The family's poverty was evident as they left the house. Father and son both wore tunics made of burlap and trousers made of cotton, and each donned a loosely fitted deerskin coat. The sacks they carried were small and made of mountain-goat hide. This was normal garb in their own village, but judging by the few traders who passed through, anywhere else in the empire they would be looked on as serfs, peasants, or even more likely, homeless. The one thing that stood out was the sword that

Will's father carried. It was similar to the sword of a soldier, double-sided and full-length. Below the cross guard the handle was white and had carvings of men taming wild beasts. The pommel was inlaid at the base with a stone in which green, blue, and purple swirled together. Will had never seen it before. Continuing to chase his father, Will noticed the sword shimmered like the small particles of blue and purple glistening on the ground.

The two men passed the giant forge where Will had planned to work his entire life. They passed by many of the other villagers' huts, mostly dark, matching the night. They passed through the old, moss-covered ruins of a giant wall. They jumped and slid from rock to rock in their descent down the steep mountainside. They drew closer and closer to the large, purple curtain enveloping their people's mountain.

Will worked hard to keep up with his father, surprised at the older man's athleticism. He managed to talk while attempting to keep the quick pace. "Dad, what is happening?"

"Will, you are the first of our people to be born without shackles. That means the curse will not hold you on this mountain. You, and only you, can pass through the curtain."

*Only me?* "You are not coming?" Will said between deep breaths.

"Will, if I try to pass through the veil I will be killed instantly. The magic will cause my heart to stop. Some have tried and no one has ever made it through with the shackles. But the traders come through no problem."

Reeling from the realization that he was going on

alone, Will asked, "What am I to do once I'm through?"

"You have to find the truth and seek to free our people."

"Why are we leaving in the middle of the night, Dad?"

"Our community is small and secluded. Word will spread quickly that you are not shackled. Somehow one of the permitted traders on our mountain will find out and the emperor will know. He will send someone to bind you like the rest of us, or maybe worse. The chief and I think it best that you escape while you are able. You will be the only one of our kind that we know of to be on the outside. We want you to have time to put distance between the mountain and yourself so that you cannot be tracked. I want you to use your hunting and trapping skills to stealthily leave this area."

"How am I supposed to free the mountain from this?" He gestured toward the giant curtain.

"That is an answer you will have to seek out. We were never permitted to learn our own history. The maps you have seen and the books you have read were all acquired through trade, but nothing tells us how to reverse our fate."

"Where do I start?"

"The traders always come from the east. I would start there."

"Is there any other way, Father? I don't want to leave you and Mom and Peran."

"For some reason, you are unique, Will. You have been blessed. We are counting on you. I wish there was another way, but I am proud that you, my son, are blessed in this way. I believe in you."

They approached the curtain. Will had never realized how confined he and his people were until this moment.

"Father, once the empire realizes I am gone, what will happen to everyone?"

"Don't trouble yourself with that thought. There are many answers to that question, and Chief Boxfen, myself, and the village elders have agreed that you getting out of this prison is more important than any of those."

Dad knelt down next to Will and fastened the sword to his waist. "This is one of the few relics we have left. We believe it is from before the Great War. As our ambassador to the world, we want you to have it to protect and defend yourself." A tear strode down his father's cheek, passing over his blue tattoo. "You are a man, Will. Be brave and do what is right. I will always be proud to call you my son, if you hold to what is right."

Will felt streams flowing down his own cheeks as he stared at his father.

"Step through the curtain, son."

Will didn't want his feet to move, but they turned and walked toward the curtain. *Stop! Don't go there! Stay here with Dad.* Despite his inner protests, that thing inside him took over and guided his feet. He looked back at his father with tears pouring over his newly revealed tattoos.

"I love you, Pop! I won't let you down. I'll come back. I'll free the village."

His father gazed at him through pools in his eyes, "May the king keep you safe, if he exists."

Will choked on his father's last words. He was halfway through the veil and he felt numb, but he managed to raise his hand and wave goodbye. His motions were sluggish within the veil, almost as if he were moving through tar.

Once through the veil, he could barely make out his father's silhouette. He saw him turn and begin the ascent. Will felt slightly faint, and he crashed to his knees in disbelief and wept. *I have no one now. No one to care for me, no one to love me. Only me, just me.* After what felt like an eternity, he remembered his father's words about getting far from the mountain. The sun was just breaking over the horizon. Using it to determine his bearing, he headed east and entered a forest he had never entered before.

As Will walked, the dust-like purple-and-blue substance surrounded him on the ground and the particles plumed out as he stepped near them. He could not actually touch the substance. He seemed to repel it at each attempt. As the sun rose, the substance became more and more translucent until Will could not see the particles at all. As he hiked deeper into the forest the undergrowth became thick. Thorn-covered plants tore at his clothes.

Exhaustion and lack sleep caused Will's mind to kick into survival mode. *Food, shelter, water. I have enough food in my pack for a couple days. The weather is temperate and should not be much of an issue. Water. Water is the key to survival.* He reflected back on the lessons his father had taught him about survival. *Go one direction until you hit water,* he'd told Will. *Once you find water, follow it until it hits a larger body of water, and then follow that downstream. This will lead to civilization.* Will knew from the maps he had seen that there should be some type of town within a couple of days hike from the mountain.

Will crossed the foothills of the Mount of Fallow. He looked up the mountainside but could not see Rand. The air tasted different from what he was used to on the mountain, and it felt lighter. The forest was full of life. He saw jackrabbits, squirrels, chipmunks, and all types of birds and other creatures. Will could have sworn that he even saw a fox, but it might have just been the way the wind was moving a branch. In the broad daylight, he saw none of the glowing substance seen the previous night. It was as if it had all disappeared, though he sensed it nearby.

Every sound put Will on high alert. Every time a squirrel waded through the leaves behind him, he thought an enemy was hunting him down. The voices of birds sometimes sounded like people, making his heart race. He began to mull over potential encounters in his head. *If I see a person, I can just play it like I am out here hunting. But what if he sees my eyes and tattoo and turns me over to the emperor? I need to find water to see if I still look the same during the daylight.* Will continued to think through all he might get himself into, whether likely or not. *If I run into a bear, I will definitely have to fight it. Block the first attack and then go for the vitals. I need to camp in an area with no way to flank me so that I can't get surrounded by wolves.* Will was ready to fight any battle that came his way. No longer a boy, he was embracing the call to arms given to him by his father and the chief.

Will traveled downhill and east until at long last he heard a creek gurgling in front of him. He slowed his approach. A short way off, Will could see the creek's surface reflecting the sunlight through some of the brush. Will paused to take in his surroundings. The creek flowed through a calm meadow. The sun was beginning to set, but the meadow was still sunny, fighting the shade of the forest like nowhere he had yet seen. He caught a glimpse of brown movement in the meadow's tall grass, a jackrabbit going toward the water. Will looked around for a weapon. *Dang, I should have grabbed my bow.* Will would not let himself be too disappointed. After all, he still had the rations from his pack. Will had never enjoyed hunting and killing animals, but he knew the necessity of it and would do so when needed. After a few minutes, he was content to enter the glade and allow the rabbit to scamper off.

*If I stay here tonight, many animals will surely visit me. There are wolf prints as well as deer, rabbit, and even bear. This means if I place traps, the other animals will get anything I catch before I do.* He looked around the glade and saw a rocky cliff about a hundred paces away. *There might be an old den or a place to make shelter up there.*

He trekked through the thick undergrowth toward the rock face. The stream he followed was very small, but it reminded him of the streams he and his friends jumped over as children on the mountain. Will approached the cliff. The water came from above, slowly cascading over the smooth rock surface. It made a small pool about a man's-height wide before running onward. He walked along the rock face looking for a crevice.

It was getting dark, and the strange blue-and-purple substance revealed itself again. *How has this substance been everywhere my entire life and I never knew of it?* He walked along the cliff wall until he came to a small cave opening. Will drew his sword just in case he had to fight a bear or a wolf. He peered into the small inlet. It was empty and seemed to have been abandoned for some time. The strange glowing substance was everywhere, revealing a small den.

The cave was about his height and twice as wide as the pool he had seen. He took off his pack. Once unbundled, he spread out the deerskin pack for use as a sleeping mat. Crashing onto the makeshift bed, his body thanked him. He reached for his now-scattered pack, pulled out some hard bread, and wolfed it down.

Will lay on his back and looked at the cave ceiling. His thoughts drifted to the drums, the fire, the knives, the tales, and the escape from the only place he wanted to be at this moment. All these thoughts swirled through his mind as he tried to make sense of them. Why hadn't his father taken time to explain the dust, or the ceremony further. Perturbed, he rolled onto his side. Face-to-face with the substance, he reached out to touch it. Just as his finger was about to make contact, it avoided him. *I can see it. Why can't I touch it?* Annoyed, he got to his knees and bent over. With his elbows bent and his hands cusped, he chased some of the purple and blue dust into itself until it had no escape. What happened next was beyond anything he could have anticipated.

# 3

As Will cupped his hands and chased the dust together, it fused into a rock. It looked similar to the stone on his sword. Confused, he reached for it and was able to grab it. It no longer ran from him. Will rolled back into a sitting position, his back rested against the cool rock wall of the cave, and he held the small stone. It seemed to sit perfectly in the palm of his hand. It was warm and light. He tossed it up, and when it came down, he caught it. He repeated this for some time. The repetition seemed to calm his troubled mind. Once his mind stopped pulsing, exhaustion got the best of him and he found sleep.

When Will woke up, it was barely dark. The stone was still beside him, glowing dimly as it had the night before. He rolled up his mat, folding it back into a pack, and got ready to go.

The day grew bright until he could not see the substance or, for that matter, his rock. After blindly fumbling around the cave floor briefly, he found it. Will held it in his hand. It was strangely transparent in the light of day. He squeezed tightly, attempting to crumble the stone made from dust, but it would not yield to his strength. He decided it was not essential for him to carry it throughout his journey, especially if he could make more. He spotted a target on the wall of the cave and hurled the rock with all his force, just for fun. As he released the rock, it felt like it disintegrated in his hand, like he was only waving his hand through the air. A split second later, however, there was a boom and a flash. The area surrounding his target was scorched with burn marks. He approached the scorched wall and put his hand on it. Spreading his fingers out, he covered the scorched surface. It was warm. He stood with his hand on the wall, stunned.

Snapping back to reality, all he wanted to do was try that again but someone might have heard the explosion. He rushed out of the cave toward the small creek and began to follow it downstream. *I made that. What was that? What am I?* The thoughts cascaded through his mind like the water rushing beside him. *What else can I do?*

The small creek slithered its way through the mountain forest. At times he had to crawl down rock faces similar to the one he'd slept in the previous night. Will fought his way under and over fallen trees. The terrain slowly became a more gradual angle and the creek widened as other small creeks merged into it.

Will saw a clearing up ahead. He crashed his way through bushes, often back-first, in order to avoid briars to the face. The thick, briary undergrowth was almost within reach of the clearing. Will closed his eye, dug his heels in and, leading with his back, he pushed.

*Splash!* Suddenly, Will was under water. He flailed for his life. The late-spring water was still cold and deadly and he didn't know how to swim. Will thrashed sporadically, trying to grip something, desperately trying to find oxygen. His feet found solid ground and he pushed off of it. Like a rocket, he shot toward the surface, leaving a trail of bubbles. Surfacing, he took a giant gulp of air. He sunk to the bottom and pushed off a few more times, slowly drawing nearer to the shore until he reached the bank.

Once on the riverbank, Will took deep breaths as he tried to blink away the stars that clouded his vision. His soaked body was cold, and his clothes were wet. He stripped down and spent a period of time wringing out his clothes and letting the sun dry them. He took the brief respite to eat his lunch. After staying as long as he dared, Will pulled on the damp but wearable clothes and took his bearings.

He had fallen into a wide river. The sight of so much water overwhelmed him. He had only ever seen small streams and creeks before. Will began to realize the world had so much to explore and many forces he had yet to encounter.

With the river slicing such a vast opening in the canopy of trees, he was able to spy the sky. The sun's position told him it was mid-afternoon, but that was not all. He saw smoke. Smoke meant people. His singular mission was to free his people, and finding civilization was the first step. Although he had not thought about what he would do once he reached it. Regardless, he knew the direction his feet must go, and he would figure it out along the way.

*I wonder if all people look like us. What will they say*

*when they see my eyes and tattoos? I can't really hide my eyes, but maybe I can wrap my face. That's what I'll do and if I go in the bright of the day, they won't notice my eyes as much.* Will took this time to examine his reflection in the slow-moving water near the bank of the river. From what he could tell, he looked normal. The tattoos were gone, and his eyes looked fine, but it was still bright. He was unsure if others would be able to see the tattoos in the dim lighting of the evening.

Will worked his way along the river. He had so many unanswered questions. He decided to camp out in the night, then approach the town in the daylight, when he was less likely to be noticed.

The smoke got closer, and he saw fishermen on rafts working the river. From what he could see, they looked like him. But still fearful of what he might look like to them, he seamlessly slipped back into the undergrowth and continued to travel out of sight.

As he approached the village, the sun was almost completely down. The glowing dust was evident on everything he saw. This definitely gave him an advantage in traveling at night. the town had one border on the river surrounded by a high wall made of vertical logs positioned side by side. They were pointed at the top. This wall surrounded the entirety of the town. There was a high cliff on the side of the town opposite that of the river. Will made his way there to find a place to sleep.

He scaled some boulders and found a nice crater to spend the night in. It offered an excellent view overlooking the town. A great fire blazed in the main square. People were singing and Will saw their silhouettes dancing around the fire. They must have been celebrating something. He heard laughter. They spoke Will's language though with a strange accent. He was relieved to know they shared a common language. That had been one of his greatest worries. He sat and watched the townspeople enjoying their time. *I wonder if I will experience such festivities, laugh and sing and be merry with those I love ever again*?

As the celebration died down, Will retired to the small area where he had laid his mat down. Once again, like the night before, he lay on his side staring at the blue-and-purple dust. The strange substance, now visible in the dark, intrigued Will. He chased it with his fingers. Playing with the substance was oddly comforting. Will scooped some together again and it again formed into the strangely warm and lightweight rock. He made another and then another. Each of them was identical and each seemed to fit into its maker's hand perfectly. Will didn't know why, but he felt connected to these rocks and passed some more time tossing a rock up in the air and catching it. After his experience earlier that morning, he knew it was risky, but he also knew that fun often involved risk.

Will took out his only extra tunic and wrapped the rocks, placing them next to his sleeping mat. He spread his deerskin jacket over himself, doubling it as a crude blanket. *Tomorrow. Tomorrow I will find something out about...*

*Chirp...chirp...chirp.* The swallow's song startled Will awake. The sun was already high in the sky. Exhaustion from the past couple of days must have finally caught up with him. He jumped up and packed his tiny campsite. He took extreme caution in packing the rocks he had made the night before. With the power they contained, the rocks could be useful if he found himself in a tight situation.

When everything was tidily packed back into the carrying sack, he climbed down the rocks that he had occupied the previous night. He crept through the woods, mostly keeping the town in sight. After about an hour he came to a road. It was time to take his first public step.

He practiced his alias in his head. *Name? Flynn. Why he was there? Searching for info on his father. Where he was from? Valkinridge. It was the ancient name of the ruined city that Rand was built on.*

As he got closer to the town, the road became busier. He saw people carrying more hay than he had ever seen. There were animals besides deer, chickens, and rabbits. His curiosity got the best of him when he saw a man traveling with a hairy, spotted creature with huge tusks in the back of his wagon. Will approached the man and said, "Excuse me, but what is that huge creature in your wagon?"

"This is a boar, son. Haven't you ever seen a boar?"

"Sorry, sir. I am not from around here." Will began to mentally kick himself. He might have given himself away.

"Say, you look familiar," the man said.

"I've never been here before."

Will tried to back away, but the man grabbed him by the shoulder, in friendly way, and stared him in the face. He was short for a fully-grown man, no taller than Will. The man was bald on top, but his arms had hair so long it flowed in the wind. He had a large belly and wore a blanched tunic that fell below his waist. Around his midsection was a thick leather belt. Attached to the belt was a scabbard, but it carried no serious weapon, only a prod he used to corral his boar.

He stared Will down for what seemed like an eternity. "What is your name, boy?"

"My name is Flynn. Flynn Lyons."

"That's a strange name. I've lived here my whole life and never heard of such a name. What are you doing in these parts?"

"I'm looking for my father. He abandoned my family when I was little." Those words tasted like bile in his mouth. What a blatant lie about the man he so adored.

At those words, the man turned a little more compassionate. "If that is the case, I would love to help you on your search. I myself was abandoned when I was young. You will come to stay with me tonight!"

"That's quite alright. I wouldn't want to be a bother to you."

Placing his arm around Will, the man smiled big and said, "I wasn't asking, kid. A boy like you in Nibridge for even one night could ruin you for life."

In an effort to remain courteous, Will accepted.

"I should at least know the name of the man to host a humble traveler such as myself."

The old man replied, "I am Felix Tanish."

# 4

Felix Tanish had lived in the valley below the mountains his entire life. He was a pig farmer by trade, but his hobby was much more interesting. He was a collector of books, primarily of ancient texts, sometimes even outlawed texts. Felix was the most educated pig farmer in all the empire.

He dressed simply, which was becoming of his profession, and for the most part, kept to himself. Most people would say he was a genuinely nice guy and fair in his dealings. Not many knew of his hobby and he was content to keep it that way. Felix had never married, and his only child was the dog, Asper, he found on the road a few years earlier.

The day Felix met Will, he had sold a few heads of boar to the butcher in Nibridge. It had been a typical Wednesday in that regard, although at the town gate there were three heavily armed strangers he did not recognize. As he got closer, he saw they bore the head of a dragon engulfing a star—the empire's crest—on their breastplates. The men had approached him and asked his name and business in town. Felix obliged them with the answers they sought. They then produced a crude drawing of a teenage boy that they said was wanted by the empire. They were offering a substantial reward for information about him. The strangers said his name was Will and that he was from a mountain town, wanted for stealing information sensitive to the empire. However, at that point, Felix could not help them.

It was on his way home that Felix came across a wild-looking boy who had asked a strange question. There were never so many foreigners in the valley of Kadis, especially in such a short time. Immediately, he thought of the reward money, but he didn't know enough about this boy. Felix never trusted the empire with what they said on the surface. They were cruel and deceiving, the lot of them. Then again, the money would allow him to retire from pig farming. He rubbed his worn knees. To retire early meant he could dedicate more time to his books and perhaps even write one.

Not knowing whether or not he would turn the boy in, Felix asked the boy to stay with him. The boy was clearly no older than sixteen or seventeen, and he appeared harmless enough. Once he had more information, he could make a decision on whether to take the empire up on its offer. In the meantime, he desperately needed help around the farm.

The old pig farmer and the young man walked side by side while the old man led the mule pulling the cart that held the remaining boar.

They approached Felix's home, which was modest for the valley, but grander than anything Will had ever seen. Will helped Felix unhook the cart and feed the animals before retiring into the house. As it got dark, Will was relieved that Felix did not appear to be able to see his blue tattoos and eyes.

The boar stew began to boil over the cast-iron pot and sizzle as it collided with the fire. The smell made Will's mouth salivate. He felt like a dog waiting for dinner scraps.

The soup was served, and Felix asked his first question. "So, Flynn, what was your father's name?"

"His name was Maxim. He was from the central part of the empire near the desert." Will ate ravenously, not paying much attention as he answered. He only focused on satisfying the gurgling emanating from his stomach.

"Maybe we have met before. Where are you from again?"

"My family lives in Valkinridge."

"Valkinridge. Hmm, do you have a large family there?"

"Not too large. Just a few brothers and sisters."

"So, Will, why did you come to the Valley Kadis instead of to the plains, or one of the cities?"

Horror struck. *How does he know my name is Will?* "Uh, my name is not Will. It's Flynn." The charade was over.

"Today I was stopped by agents of the empire looking for a boy named Will with a sketch that looked like you, my boy. Now I have no love for the empire, but they are offering a large reward for you. What is it you have done to them that they are willing to pay so much?"

Will kept silent.

Felix tried a different approach, "Why did you say you were from Valkinridge? Don't you know that place is forsaken and has resided in the forbidden territory for over two hundred years?"

Surprised, Will decided to be honest and pray the man didn't turn him in. "I had no idea about the forbidden territory, but Valkinridge is not forsaken. There is a village called Rand. My people live there."

Felix looked stunned. He said, "From what I'ver heard, the empire kills anyone immediately that is found trespassing in the forbidden territory. No trial, no tribune. It is a death sentence to go there. Why would they let your people reside there?"

Will told him of the events of the night of his birthday, and of his people's dealing with the empire. He intentionally left out the business with the purple-and-blue dust, as well as the tattoos and blue eyes, especially since it was dark, and Felix didn't seem able to see them.

As Will finished recounting the events of his journey, leaving out the part about the exploding stones, Felix seemed to have made up his mind.

"Will Merle's-son, you are safe with me. It is a blessing we ran into each other. I may be able to tell you some of your history and that of the empire. But not tonight. We have spoken much, and I want some time to process this information. Please let us continue after a good night's rest."

Felix showed Will to his room. Once the door was shut, Will grabbed his bag and considered running away, but instead sat on the bed. He contemplated his situation bitterly. He had not even made it to the city and had blown everything. His life and the hope of his people rested on this stranger keeping Will's secret. The feeling of failure weighed down on him like a millstone. After a minute he pulled himself together. He unpacked some of his rocks and stationed them on his nightstand. If he had to fight his way out, he would be able to reach them quickly. As he lay in bed, he thought of what the empire might do if they recaptured him. He'd made vows to not be taken alive, to fight until his last breath. Eventually, the emotions of the day and the soft bed got to him, and he drifted to the land of dreams.

Once Will was in his room, Felix attended to his desk. He pulled out blank parchment and inked Will's story down, careful to be vague in case the empire searched his house. He was keenly aware that harboring Will was asking for trouble from the empire. But he wanted to record what he'd heard before he forgot the details. Someday it could make an excellent addition to his collection.

The light of dawn broke through the window. It must have only been a few minutes later when Felix opened the door.

"Get up, Will! We are burning daylight!"

"Are you going to tell me anymore about my people's history?"

"Your lessons will begin after the sun goes down tonight, Will."

"Then why are we awake?"

"If you are going to stay here, you must earn your keep. I am getting old and it will do me well to have some young blood around here."

Will knew it was only right for him to help. "Alright, Felix. I'll work, you teach. I'll be down in a minute."

Felix left as Will crawled out of his bed. Once

breakfast was finished, the work began. Luckily for Will, swine farming was not a difficult task to learn. Although it was easy to pick up, it was messy and hard work. After doing the feedings, Will learned to wrangle. The toughest job was probably digging a new trench from a spring-fed pond to the farm. The old man had been carrying buckets for a few years, he'd said, and his back would not co-operate with digging the trench himself.

As the sun began to set, it would have been hard to tell the difference between Will and one of the pigs. The filth and the stench would have overcome most men. Felix led Will to the pond and instructed him to bathe and then come in for dinner. That night they once again had pork stew.

As Will cleaned up from dinner, Felix stole to the other room to his writing desk. He pushed the desk from its usual resting place, then took a slim iron bar and slid it between two floorboards. As he pried, the board squeaked softly and then snapped upwards.

"Is everything alright, Felix?" Will called from the other room.

"Everything is great!" Felix replied. He slipped his hand into the hole, searching in the darkness. When he felt the soft leather of goatskin, he grabbed on. Clasping the book by the spine, he pulled it from its hiding spot.

As soon as dishes were done, Will sat down at the table, exhausted. He stared into the fire and his eyelids drooped. The dancing flames reminded him of the celebrations and dancing that he had once enjoyed in Rand.

*Wham!* Will jumped and fell out of his chair backward. As he climbed back to his feet, he realized what caused the sound. Felix had slammed a book on the table. He stood there smiling at Will's embarrassment.

The book was bound in a light-brown hide. It had scorch marks on it, as if it had been rescued from a fire. The pages looked aged and yellow, and Will thought he could smell a musk emanating from them. Across the front, the book was titled *The Origin of the Blue and Red Eyes.*

When Will saw the title, his stomach jumped. He could feel the wild thing inside him as his heart beat heavily. Will thought of the village men, and of himself, when he saw the words *Blue Eyes*. He started to speak, but his mouth felt full of cotton.

Again, he tried, "What is this book?"

"This, Will, is an incredibly dangerous book. The empire would burn us alive just for having it."

"Why is it dangerous?" Will replied.

Felix continued. "Because it holds the truth. It tells why the world is the way it is. It tells of things the empire doesn't want any civilian to know." Felix turned from the cover to the first page. The ancient smell of the old book filled the air. He inhaled deeply through his nostrils and let out a slight ahh.

The first page was a charcoal sketch. It depicted what looked like two humans, but they were winged. Their hands were locked. Clearly, each was struggling to overcome the other. The one on the left had the same tattoos as all the men in Will's village. Even more disturbing, the winged man with his chiseled jaw and slightly narrow eyes looked an almost spitting image of Will's father.

On the right was an unfamiliar creature, another winged person with three small horns protruding from his forehead. The tattoos on his face were not smooth and symmetrical like those of the villagers. They looked like scars left from being savaged by a large, clawed animal. The unfamiliar tattoos were jagged and unsightly, spanning the being's face and body. Most disturbing was the maimed-looking man's wicked smile—a smile that would haunt the nightmares of children; a smile that would instill fear in the heart of any man who saw it; a smile that would enjoy the suffering its master caused others.

Will felt a tremor travel up his spine. The tremor stemmed not from fear, but from the wild thing deep inside him. The image of the beast on the right made Will want to run. Run and find this creature. To hunt it down and end it. He had never felt like this. Will was stunned by his own thoughts. It felt as if some great injustice had been done, and the only way forward was to do battle with that creature.

"What are these things?" Will asked, turning his gaze from the page.

"What you see here are two Valkyns. More specifically, they are Macceus on the left and Lushian on the right." Felix turned the page.

Another sketch, this time of a man. Truth be told, he looked more mountain than man. He was large, athletically built, and carried an enormous hammer.

"This is the Eternal King. No one knows his true name, because he never gave it to us. This king tamed our lands and used to rule over it." He flipped back to the first page. "These two were his second and third in command. They answered only to the king. Macceus was second and Lushian was third. They worked to keep evil from invading our land. They fended off the enemies of the land who would want to rule over us, keeping us free. They would lead their legions and always had victory, never failing to keep evil away. However, as the tale goes, one day they were out patrolling the mountains of the north by air when they came across a warrior dressed in complete darkness."

Felix flipped to another page and showed it to Will. It was a picture of a warrior wearing a helmet with only two eye slits. It seemed odd that there was no hole for breathing. He was armored with a large shield bearing the empire's crest. After taking in the picture, Felix flipped the pages back to the picture of the two Valkyns and continued the history lesson. "The two Valkyns stopped to speak with the imposing figure.

"'What is your business in our kingdom?' Macceus asked.

"The stranger answered, 'I have come to conquer and rule over this land.'

"At this, Macceus drew his sword. The dark warrior raised his arm and motioned with his hand toward Macceus's sword and it became like molten lead in his hand. He dropped it, stunned.

"Enamored, Lushian asked, 'What are you?'

"The dark warrior answered, 'I am the future. I am power. I am might. Follow me and you will be second only to me in the new empire. We will rule together. I will make you a god.'

"Macceus lunged and tackled the warrior. He grabbed a hidden dagger from his ankle and attempted to plunge it into the stranger's heart.

Macceus knew that this would-be usurper must be stopped. But as the dagger dove toward the despot's heart, a hand restrained him. Macceus looked from the hand up and saw a familiar face. Lushian had betrayed not only his brother but his kingdom and their king. The two began to exchange metallic strikes as they flew, encircling one another.

"'Lushian! What have you done?' Macceus yelled over the sound of the blades singing.

"'You heard what the man said, Macceus! We could be gods over this land. We would no longer need to serve. We would be rulers. We would be the icons of worship!'

"'You would betray your king?' Macceus asked indignantly.

" 'I have.'

"The dueling now switched from glancing blows to fatal combat, each looking to score a mortal wound. Macceus had but a small blade while Lushian still had a full-sized sword. Lushian with a clear advantage drove Macceus to the ground through a series of heavy chopping strikes. It was all Macceus could do to block the strikes with his small dagger. Once they landed, the dark warrior snuck behind Macceus and broke his wing.

"Outnumbered and cornered at the edge of a cliff face, Macceus had two options: fight and die, hoping to take the two with him in death, or retreat and warn the king of the betrayal and the new enemies. Macceus weighed the odds and dove off the cliff into the water below. That is said to be the last time that Lushian was seen with blue eyes. Henceforth, he always appeared with his horns and red scars and red eyes. It is said that as the emperor and his desires corrupted him, he became what he looked like in his heart, a monster. A Valkyn's appearance is not fixed, Will, but changes with his heart."

Abruptly, Felix declared, "It is already late. We can go over more tomorrow."

Will had been engrossed in the fantastic tale. He protested the old man's decision. "Tell me more, Felix. I can stay up. I promise. Please?"

Felix looked at the young man with a gentle but firm expression. "Will, we have more time to learn tomorrow night. We have another early morning."

Will respectfully conceded, knowing the man was right. They needed rest for the hard labor on the farm. They bid each other goodnight and went off to bed.

Will dreamed of flying as the birds of the air flew. Flying how he imagined Macceus would have flown in the story.

# 5

After a long day of chores, the two once again began their lesson.

"Tonight, can we learn more about the Valkyns?" Will asked.

Felix flipped to a page in the now familiar book. The chapter title "Valkinridge" appeared. Felix smirked at Will's stunned facial expression and began the lesson.

"There is not much known about the Valkyns' origins. All that is known is that when the king tamed the land, the Valkyns were with him. As we ordinary folk began to inhabit the land, the Valkyns built Valkinridge. It was their haven and primary living dwelling."

"Is there anything special about the Valkyns besides their wings?" Will interrupted.

"Well, it is said they have the ability to manipulate magic."

"Magic?"

Felix continued. "It is said that magic is everywhere in our land; however, that seems to be a baseless claim and impossible to prove. If it was here, wouldn't we be able to see it?"

Will thought about how at this very moment he could see a purple and blue powdery substance residing in the places the fire was not illuminating.

Will smiled delightedly as Felix continued. "However, it has been recorded that the Valkyns would often stave off an attack by using fire shot out of their hands."

Will thought back to the rocks he had formed, sitting at this moment in his room. *Am I a Valkyn? It would all add up if I am. But I can't fly. I don't have wings.*

The lesson carried on, but it was mostly Felix just imagining what it would be like to fly and use magic. Will thought back to the eagles on the mountain and indulged himself in the same fantasy of flight.

"Felix, do you have any books on the Valkyns, specifically, that I could study?"

"I only have one. Since you are from Valkinridge, I feel as though I can entrust its protection to you."

Felix retrieved a slim book titled *An Outsider's Understanding of Valkyns.* He handed it to Will.

Will began to ask questions about it, but it was late, and the old man was once again resolute about the need for sleep.

That night Will slept holding the book in his arms. He dreamed of the epic battles of Macceus and Lushian that were so fresh in his mind.

Wake. Eat. Work. Eat. Lesson. Sleep. This was the pattern Will followed for the next few days. He learned that Macceus had made it back to the king to warn him of the invader and of the bitter betrayal of

Lushian. He learned that Lushian snuck back into the kingdom and deceived a large number of Valkyns to follow him, and that there were a thousand years between the betrayal of Lushian and the Great War.

Will was on the edge of his seat every lesson, avidly listening and learning. Felix confirmed that the home of the Valkyns, Valkynridge, was located on the Mount of Fallow and that it was in those ruins Will had played. These remnants were of the Valkyns' main dwelling place within the kingdom.

"Ahh..." Felix let out a satisfied sound.

"Ugh," Will replied, as they finished their usual dinner of pork stew.

"Tonight, we will learn of the Great War."

"Would you like me to get the book?" asked Will. Felix had trusted Will with the secret of its hiding place.

"No, no. This story has never been allowed to be recorded. It has been said that to do so would dishonor the memory of the men and Valkyns who fought."

"I see. I'll stoke the fire then."

Once Will had a nice fire blazing, Felix began. "It had been a thousand years since the betrayal. Lushian and the emperor began an elaborate plot to overthrow the monarchy. Initially, they used disinformation as their primary weapon."

Will knew the power of words from his own studies.

"They disseminated lies about the king, saying he sought to make his citizens slaves. They portrayed the Valkyns who had always fought for the good of the kingdom as corrupt tyrants. In contrast, the emperor and his allies talked of their own greatness and how they would free the people from tyranny and strengthen them with imperial power. They slowly won people to their cause and began to build their armies.

The emperor led the legions of men, and Lushian led the Valkyns who had turned. They sent operatives into the cities to cause dissent. Riots broke out. When Macceus and his Valkyns came to restore peace, the townspeople threw rotten food and attempted to capture them. The people fully bought into the simple but strong lie. They believed that, somehow, they had been wronged. They believed they were a victim of the Eternal King's reign. But, the most ruthless thing the emperor and Lushian did was to pay a price for each Valkyn wing that someone brought to them."

Will gasped at this last piece of information. Not only did wings enable the Valkyns to fly, but from his other readings he had learned that if their wings were removed, they ceased to be immortal. This made the decree all the more abominable.

"One of the worst tragedies in the history of our land happened as a result of this directive. One night when Valkinridge was asleep, a band of mercenaries snuck in. They found Macceus sleeping, and they struck him before he could fight back. After knocking him unconscious, they bound him and cleaved off his wings. He eventually was able to break free and laid waste to the intruders, but it was too late. Lushian's evil plan had worked. People started riots simply to lure the Valkyns in so they could capture them and cut off their wings. The people wanted the reward, and they even thought they were doing a service for the good of all people.

"Eventually, the Valkyns stopped responding and violence spread. The violence resulted in higher crime and suffering. In their suffering, the people wrongly accused the king of the devastation caused by the emperor and Lushian. The king continued to rule justly and well, but the people rebuffed established laws and catered to the imperial sentiment.

"At this point, the emperor and Lushian declared an all-out war. The empire no longer fought in the shadows but came in force. There were many battles, both between men and Valkyns. Lushian's Valkyns had a clear advantage. He and his legion of Valkyns still could fly while only a few of those in Macceus's legion still had their wings. Outmatched, they had no option but to retreat and fight another day. The Eternal King fought and conquered. No one could stand up to him. Though he fought for the people and the kingdom, a just cause, even more people turned on him. They stopped believing the king would win. Eventually, the people started to cheer for Lushian and the emperor's victories. The king's troops could no longer find lodging, and food was sparse.

"When the king saw that the people no longer desired the kingdom he had established and protected for them, and that they had rejected the king himself, he met with Macceus. They decided that they would allow the people to have their choice of ruler. He had no desire to fight the people he had loved so much. If the people so hated the king and his Valkyns for doing what they knew was right, then they would bide their time and wait for a chance to redeem the people and the land. The people of the land betrayed their king and betrayed those who had faithfully served them.

"The king disbanded his army, desiring for brother to fight brother no longer. He turned himself and his legion of Valkyns over to Lushian and the emperor. Once in the hands of the empire, they were dealt with cruelly, despite specific terms of surrender. The king was bound with magic chains inside of a mountain prison. When the Valkyns surrendered, most were slaughtered after laying down their arms. The empire left only a small wingless population alive and forced them to work metal. The Valkyns had a particular gift in working metals..."

"From there, the Emperor conquered the coastal kingdom which had been isolated city states."

# 6

It had been a couple weeks since Will arrived. Felix appreciated the help on the farm and the ability to teach someone all he had learned from his years of poring over books. Will seemed grateful for the roof over his head. More than that, they had developed a genuine and mutual trust. They had become friends.

Felix went to Nibridge on his usual market day and delivered the desired number of boars to the butcher, but this day something seemed off. A number of large carriages that he had not seen before sat just outside the wooden city walls. Once through the city gate, there was at least a squadron, if not two, of imperial troops combing through the streets, looking behind every barrel and piece of debris. *The carriages are troop transporters.* The troops were searching houses with little regard for their owners' possessions. Felix tried to stroll casually through the main square, but was quickly cornered. Luckily, the local constable, an old friend, accompanied the harassing troops and vouched for Felix.

Felix was able to keep his cool and avoid the

soldiers the rest of the time in town. It was a tremendous feat to not show his anxiousness on the return home. Once he had the opportunity, he was off. Felix knew his risk for housing Will was growing. *How much longer can I keep him hidden? He is going to get me strung up!* These thoughts troubled him as he rushed home.

Felix opened the worn door and walked across the threshold. The scene he witnessed filled him with pride. Will had dinner, pork stew, already on the table waiting. Next to the stew there was a map sprawled out on the table. Will had been diligently studying it up until the time that Felix returned home.

"What is happening here?" Felix asked.

"I am trying to figure out where everything you have been teaching me has happened," Will said, smiling as he looked up at Felix.

"Well, show me what you have discovered."

Will pointed to a mountain range on the east side of the map.

"This where we are, and here is my mountain. Over here." He pointed to a large spacious area. "This is the desert of Miklak." He moved his hand to the north, pointing to another mountain range. "This is where the Great Betrayal happened." Moving toward the south, "This is the Dark Forest. We haven't discussed it, but it's labeled." Will pointed to two cities labeled *Fizon* and *Tizon* on the far west side of the map. "These are the river cities, Tizon is the capital of the empire and just outside Tizon, in the Miklak Desert, is the King's Mountain." His index finger rested on this point for a few moments. Will lowered his voice to almost whisper and said,

"This is where the king is imprisoned."

Felix's heart swelled. He felt like a father whose son just caught his first fish or harvested his first deer. This made his news all the more heartbreaking.

"I am so proud of you, Will. I couldn't have asked for a better student or friend. However, I don't think you can stay much longer." Tears burned Felix's eyes as the words came out.

Will winced at the verbal dagger. He asked why.

Felix sadly responded, "I want you to stay, but for your own safety you need to leave. The empire has stepped up their search efforts for you. You are more likely to be found if you stay."

Felix could tell his explanation wasn't helping. He went on, "You will always be welcome in my house, and you can stay a few more days. After that, I think for your own good you should be on your way."

Every word Felix said stemmed from a truth inside himself. On his walk home, he had recognized that he would do anything to protect the young man who had become his closest friend and confidant. That even meant asking him to leave.

Will sat and, with watery eyes, watched the fire. If he said anything, he would justify the new wound inside him. The silence was hard and mean. It forced Will to recognize the reality of his situation. *How can Felix do this to me? Had I really thought I could live here forever?* The questions in Will's thoughts brought him to the realization that even if he wanted to sneak away and live an isolated life, the empire would never stop searching for him. Based on his conversations with Felix, he had deduced he was some remnant of the ancient Valkyns who the emperor had spared at the end of the Great War. Without saying a word, Will stood and strode over to Felix and clapped him twice on the shoulder as if to say, "I understand." He then walked out of the room and up the stairs.

Will tossed and turned in bed as, he recounted the conversation. He understood Felix's reasoning but it still made him angry. His strong will burned with frustration at the situation. Just then, Will heard the distant clopping of a horse. It grew louder and joined with the sound of many horses and a carriage.

His heart raced as he got out of bed. Through the window and saw a mass of torches burning. The torches were quickly approaching the house. The carriers must have been on horseback. He grabbed his pack of belongings.

Felix burst in. "Will, the empire is here! You have to get out. Run! Go to the Dark Forest. You may find sanctuary there. The empire loathes going there." He grabbed Will by the shoulders and looked sternly into his eyes. "Will, you were chosen for something great. Don't ever believe you aren't worthy of the task you are called to carry out. I want you to take this." He handed Will a small parchment.

"This is a map for your travels." Felix turned toward the doorway. He looked over his shoulder, glanced down at the floor, and then back to Will. He spoke in an almost inaudible whisper, "Please come visit me again." And he was gone.

Will never had a chance to say a word. Just like the last time he had seen his dad. *I can't think about that now. I have to get out!* Will shouldered his pack the rest of the way.

*Knock, knock, knock!* "Open up!"

He heard Felix's feet scuffling toward the door. The window was his only option. He looked out. Soldiers were congregated primarily at the door, but were beginning to fan out to surround the house.

*Now or never.* Will leaped out of the second story window and landed softly on the boar cart. He stole away into the surrounding cornfield.

Will burst out of the field and onto the road. As he looked back, he saw soldiers entering Felix's house. There was something odd in the sky above Felix's house. He stopped and peered. At first it looked like flames. His eyes focused after a few seconds and he realized it was something flying. It was a Valkyn!

Its red eyes now locked onto his own. As they momentarily stared at each other, Will's eyes felt cold. A righteous indignation rose up within him. The Valkyn flew high and then, like a hawk, dived for him. Will pulled one of the magic rocks out of his trouser pocket. *Wait.* The Valkyn was getting closer. *Wait.* It flew within a couple body lengths. Will took aim and, with all his might, threw the stone at the beast.

There was an explosion. A direct hit. The Valkyn crumpled to the ground, writhing in pain. Will wanted to continue to fight, wanting to end the traitor, but by this point, the soldiers had surely seen. Will stole back into the field and ran toward the mountains. He ran until his lungs wouldn't allow him to run anymore. The cool air burned with every inhalation. He caught the scent of smoke. Only then did he look back and see that the soldiers had set the fields ablaze.

It was all he could do not to think of what they might do to Felix. Will had to stay focused. He thought of the map. He must follow the mountains to the Dark Forest. Will began to hear voices through the lingering smoke. He had dawdled too long. With the mountains as his guide, he took off again.

Will reached the foothills. As he climbed the somewhat more familiar terrain than the valley, Will leaped from rock to rock, scaling the boulders at an almost inhuman speed. He had played on rocky slopes his entire life. Soldiers in full gear wouldn't have the dexterity to climb after him. That didn't slow him down, though. He knew a Valkyn didn't have to climb up the rock face. To make matters worse, he knew his tattoos and eyes glowed bright blue in the night, and a Valkyn would be able to see him as easily as he had seen the one over Felix's house. He was a blue beacon in the night.

Will ran and climbed. The morning sun was starting to break the horizon as he pushed through thick undergrowth. He shoved to get through the heavy brush, and tripped and fell, landing with a definitive *thud* next to a stream. Not able to muster the strength to stand, he moved his face near to the water and sipped the cool, soothing liquid.

Will was covered, from an aerial view, by the thick brush of the marshy foothills of the Eastern Mountains. He was invisible from the air and no group of men would dare follow him through the marsh, which was exactly why he had gone in. The cool mountain-fed spring was his only friend, and what a friend it was—healing and ministering to him in his exhausted state.

Will took his pack off and hung it on a nearby

branch. Then, like one of the swine he had taken care of, he rolled onto his back, submerging himself in mud and water. Will looked up to the bright blue skies. There was little cloud cover. The birds were singing. His stomach let out a loud gurgle almost as if trying to join the birdsong. He looked in his pack, hopeful, but realized he had nothing to eat. As his head rested in the watery mud his thoughts began to crystallize. He could either follow the stream out of the foothills to a larger body of water in search of a meal or he could try his hand at foraging and hunting the bog.

The bog was teeming with food. As he observed his surrounding, he saw cattails close by. Once he regained his composure, he made a beeline for the cattails. He dug some of the roots up and set them aside. Next, he pulled a small metal bowl out of his pack, a gift from Felix, and placed some water in it. Will then sliced some of the roots up into bite-size pieces and poured them in. All that was needed to finish his simple stew was to bring it to a boil. He had an idea for starting the fire.

Will took two of the magical rocks out of his backpack. His idea was to strike the two together and hopefully create a spark. To test his theory while keeping his hands attached to his body, he struck them together underwater There was a rush of bubbles and the rocks became warm, but they did not explode. He stacked up some dry twigs and made a spot for his cup to heat once there was a fire. The moment of truth came when he struck the rocks toward the fire and sparks flew off the rocks. It was as if the sparks were a handful of sand. There were so many that they rained fire on the kindling and the small cooking fire was started easily.

Will ate the bland cattail stew. Truthfully, he would have preferred the pork stew he had eaten so much of. After his stomach was full, he had to get out of the bog and find a dry place to sleep. He chose to go uphill into the familiar mountainous terrain.

Will pulled his pack on and began following the creek toward the mountains. He was able to find some deer trails, which he used to navigate his way through the mire. Will knew he could not camp out in the open. He feared being caught asleep by one of those devilish Valkyn he had attacked earlier. They at least could see his eyes and the tattoos on his face. As the sun was waning, he found a large tree that had fallen over. Will took the remaining daylight to stack sticks up on either side, creating a small enclosure. He sprawled the deerskin out on the ground, creating a barrier with the earth, and then crawled into his quaint dwelling.

It was not as dark as it would be for normal folks. Everywhere he saw the glowing powder. He managed to compress some into a few more stones to replenish the ones he had used. He now saw it as vital to keep a small stock of stones. After his resupply, he performed the soothing technique of tossing one up and catching it. This simple exercise brought peace and clarity to him. But a troubling thought kept sleep at bay, *What are they doing to Felix?*

# 7

The pounding on the door was so vicious it about popped the hinges from the frame. Felix opened the door, fully conscious of the fact that his life could end the next moment. *At least I will die having saved Will from these monsters.* In one motion Felix slipped the deadbolt from its fastened position and the door burst open.

Instantly, Felix felt a constricting pressure and then a thump to the back of his head. The first soldier through had grabbed his throat and thrust him up against a wall.

*"Where is the boy!"* the soldier shouted.

"You're mistaken. There is no boy here..." Felix struggled to say as he gasped for breath. The soldier tightened his grip and the edges of Felix's vision begin to fade. The only thing that he could clearly see was the soldier's face, or at least where it would have been. The soldiers wore black leather masks that covered their whole faces. Every mask had a hole for each eye, and one for the mouth. Where the nose would have been, there were small slits cut to allow airflow.

The mask came close, and Felix could see the brutish soldier's green pupils. The man hissed his threat, "If we find so much as a hair that doesn't belong to you, we will make you wish you were dead."

As if Felix weighed not much more than a child, the soldier lifted him off the ground and threw him aside. Felix crumpled like a rag doll as he crashed into the hard, wooden floor.

Regaining his breath and fortitude, he backed into the nearest wall as more soldiers filed in to search his home. All of the other soldiers seemed to report back to the first soldier who had assaulted Felix.

"Commander, there are multiple rooms that were being occupied," a soldier reported.

"Is that so?" The commander glared at Felix.

The commander began to walk toward the weakened old man. "Well, Felix, it seems that you have been harboring an enemy of the empire." A cruel smile shown through the mouth opening in the masked face. "We have a particularly excruciating way to deal with traitors. We—"

Another soldier burst into the room. "Commander! The boy attacked the Valkyn, he is hurt pretty bad. We need reinforcements on the roads right now!"

The commander let out an irked snarl. "Everyone out!" he ordered to those still rummaging through the house.

"Reigns, take the prisoner and transport him to the northeast barracks, but before you do, treat him to some fireworks. Let's go!"

Reigns walked up to Felix and asked, "Will you walk or do you prefer to be dragged?" The question was so nonchalant that Felix truly believed the soldier did not care which option he chose.

"I-I will walk. Just let me grab—"

Reigns interrupted, "You will not be permitted any belongings."

Reigns guided Felix to the door and then outside. Once outside, smoke stung Felix's eyes. The fields all around were burning. *What do they think Will is capable of if they are willing to go to these lengths to capture him?*

"Light it up!" Reigns shouted.

At his command, two soldiers walked toward Felix's house with torches blazing.

Realization sunk in. "No, no!" shouted Felix. *My books!* He turned to Reigns. "Please, no! Don't do this! My books are in there."

Seemingly indifferent to his pleas, Reigns responded, "You won't need books where you are going."

Felix tried to rush toward the house to stop the soldiers, but Reigns easily caught him and, using his elbow, quickly incapacitated him with a swift hit to the temple.

When Felix woke up, he was no longer outdoors, instead he was in a dark, musty room. He tried to touch his throbbing temple, but his hands were bound. His feet were fastened to the chair he was now seated in. As his vision became clear, he realized it was not a room, but a cell carved out of stone. A single candle burned next to the gated entrance where a man sat in a chair watching him.

"Where am I?" Felix inquired, trying to seem pleasant.

The man looked at him quizzically and, ignoring

Felix's question, asked his own. "What did you do that the emperor himself is coming to see you?"

# 8

Will's sleep was restless at best. Once morning broke, he crawled out from his hovel. His clothes were still not dry. He went about his duties in his undergarments. He set snare traps across some small-game tracks. He gathered kindling and cooked another bland cattail stew.

When the sun was at high noon, his clothes were finally dry enough to travel. He checked his snares and to his delight, he had caught a jackrabbit. After cleaning and quartering his rabbit, he stored it in his pack. The sun was beginning its descent to the west from its highest position. It was time to start moving again. Dry clothes had cost him precious distance from those who pursued him.

Travel was much the same as it had been the day before. He pressed on through the miry terrain, following trails made by animals. Every once in a while, he stepped on ground that looked solid, but ended up being a pitfall and soaked his leg. Slowly the bog turned back into rocky foothills as he continued his journey south.

Will traveled as late as he dared. He was able to

build another lean-to shelter, but by the time the shelter was complete, daylight was gone.He had to set traps and cook in the dark. He once again ate cattail stew, but this time with bits of rabbit. He dried most of the rabbit by hanging it in the smoke above the fire so that it would keep longer. He curled up on his deer hide and drifted off to sleep.

In his dream, he stood before the Eternal King. The king called to him, "Will, come to me."

Will replied, "I cannot. The empire is searching for me and I would surely be caught on my way."

The king repeated, "Will, come to me."

On and on it went as Will gave the king legitimate excuse after legitimate excuse only for him to reply, "Will, come to me."

Will woke up with his veins pulsing. His frustration with the king had raised his heart rate. *Why wouldn't he just listen to me? It doesn't make sense for me to go there. I'm running for my life.*

Dawn was breaking. Will reasoned that his dream was just that, a dream. He had bigger priorities today, like getting to the Dark Woods. He checked his traps. Nothing. He shouldered his pack and placed a few magic rocks in his pockets. As he took his first step of the day, a blood-curdling howl broke through the quiet morning.

Will jerked his head to look over his shoulder as his heart began to drum. *HOOOWWWL!* It came again, sounding closer. He heard a man's voice but couldn't make it out. Will began to sprint. It was like playing tag when he was younger, only the consequences would be much worse if he got caught.

Will ducked under branches as he weaved between the trees. The howling was getting closer.

"You can't hide from me, boy," a voice called.

Will came to a steep hill and, without stopping, he stretched his leg out, landing on his hip and sliding down the hillside. After his quick descent, he stole a glance at the crest of the hill. An animal larger than any wolf he had ever seen stared back at him with eyes that could only make him think of death. The beast had black-and-gray fur, but also many bald patches, as if from previous battles.

The beast ran down the hill. Will ran along the base of the hill as the creature gained ground. As Will rounded a bend, he came face to face with a sheer rock cliff. The animal had him cornered! He heard the heavy breathing of the animal even as he gasped for his own oxygen. Baring its teeth, the creature began to drool. Will felt the wildness inside him course through his body. It burned like cool fire as it surged through his veins.

Faced with the option of death or a fight for his life, Will held no fear. Fighting was the only choice. He was destined for this. In one motion, Will dropped his traveling pack and grabbed a stone from his pocket.

The creature stood still, waiting for its master. Will launched the rock at the beast. The creature simply sidestepped. *How did he see that?* Will thought it must be luck. He wailed another rock. Again the creature sidestepped, and the explosion of the rock hit a tree behind it. The creature drew closer, forcing Will closer to the rock face.

Will threw rock after rock. The beast easily dodged each one as if it were merely toying with him. Will stepped back, grabbed his pack, and drew the sword given to him by his father. As he pointed it at the beast, the sun caught the gemstone forged into the handle. This sent the wolf-creature into a tantrum. It pounded the ground with its paws and growled.

The beast lunged at Will. He barely dodged the animal and swung his sword like a wild man. Will didn't even come close to grazing the beast. The wolf rounded on him and prepared to launch another attack. Will's only experience with a sword had been playing war with sticks with the other children in the village. He knew the wolf was cunning. He had to be creative to kill it. It lunged again and once again Will barely evaded. Will noticed a rock on the ground. He backed toward the small obstacle as the wolf got closer. When he was almost on top of it, he intentionally knocked his foot against the rock and fell backward.

The giant wolf jumped and landed on Will, cutting its sharp claws into his shoulders, digging deeply into flesh. As Will stared the beast in the eyes, he saw the animal's life-light depart. In the instant when the creature lept Will fell and the animal was airborne, Will had inverted his sword, causing it to impale itself onto the sword.

The beast fell heavily on Will, knocking the breath out of him. Will rolled it off him. He was covered in the beast's sticky blood. He climbed to his knees, taking deep breaths. He knew he had to keep moving. His body, fueled only by adrenaline, moved toward his pack. As Will shouldered the pack, he felt the cuts from the wolf's claws pulsing underneath the pack's weight. He prepared himself and took one last look. *It really isn't that scary no—*

*HOOOWWL!*

Will jumped back and his stomach nearly leapt out of his throat. *Howl!* It wasn't this wolf...there must be more.

"We are on him now, boys! Go, go, go!" It was the same voice again.

Will took off running. He continued along the rock face until he came to a clearly worn path. The path was declining toward an ancient, eerie-looking forest. *That must be the Dark Forest.*

*HOOOWWL!*

Will ran toward the forest. Every so often he glanced back. The third time he dared to look back, he saw two more black beasts break onto the trail from the thick brush. He pushed himself harder. Every breath was painful. It was as if he breathed in ice with every inhalation.

Will looked back again. Four beasts now, and behind them, a man. At the sight of him, Will burned with hatred. If he wasn't so vastly outnumbered, he might have turned back to try and fight him. Will was close to the forest now, but the beasts had gained ground. They were almost on him. The trees grew larger. They were tall, strong-looking trees with strange carvings on them, unlike the pines he had known growing up in the mountains. The beasts were almost on his heels. *Almost there.* He sprinted into the forest.

As soon as Will ran past the strange carvings, he felt a gust of wind and heard whimpering from the beasts. They stood just on the other side of the entrance to the forest, crying and gnashing their teeth.

The man called out, "I will find you, and when I do, I will end this!"

Will paused, placing his hands on his knees, confused as he looked back. For some reason, the man and wolves had stopped and did not enter the forest. Though Will assumed they could not, he was risking nothing and continued sprinting. If he had crossed the threshold to the forest a moment or two later, the beasts would have taken him.

When Will reached what he felt was a sufficient distance from his enemies, he leaned against a tree and slid down, the bark tugging on his back as it brushed by. Sitting there, he placed his hands on his head, closed his eyes, and breathed deeply. His chest rolled with the deep breaths. After he caught his breath, he looked around trying to get his bearings. He was still on a trail of some sort, running along a large creek. The presence of this creek made him realize the dryness in his mouth and throat.

A worn path led to the water's edge. On the bank, two trees had grown up and intertwined, forming an arch. Will stumbled toward it with sore, clunky legs. He kneeled down in the water and drank, staying to let the chilled water revive him and soothe his aching legs. After feeling some of his strength return, he proceeded to the bank and ate the smoked rabbit. It was tough and chewy, but the smoke had given it a delicious taste that made his mouth water. Will was ravenous. He built a small fire and cooked the remaining cattails. As he ate, Will thought of eating pork stew and talking with Felix. The happiness from the memory and the idea of what might have happened to Felix caused a tear to slowly trail down his face.

A full stomach and hydration helped restore Will

to his senses. In his mind, he reasoned that he was safe. *For some reason those demonic wolves cannot enter this forest. But why? What do they fear?* He felt uneasy, beginning to sense that he was being watched. More than once, he turned his head quickly to try and catch someone spying on him, but no one was there.

The sun began to set, and Will began to see the magic dust. The river glowed blue as it passed. The sight was breathtaking. The light from the fire shown on Will's shirt. He was covered in blood, not only his own but also the wolf's. Will removed his tunic. It stung as he peeled the shirt off his shoulders, reopening the wounds. He also removed his trousers. It had been too long since he had a real cleaning. Only in his undergarments he walked out into the creek and sat. Will scrubbed his tattered tunic and pants. Once clean enough, he hung them on some tree branches. He went back into the stream a few steps and kneeled. The cold water felt refreshing as he rubbed the coldness into his wounds and face. Will was almost clean when he again got that sneaking suspicion that someone was looking at him.

A feminine voice spoke. "Hello, Angel."

# 9

Reigns carried the heavy, incapacitated Felix into the barracks. Once inside, a small, mouse-like man who Reigns knew was the barrack clerk, addressed him,

"Take him to Ambros, He is to be on the first wagon out of here. The emperor wants to see him."

Reigns responded, "Yes, sir." He carried the limp body of Felix to the stables where he met up with Ambros.

"So this is the accomplice?" Ambros asked, raising an eyebrow skeptically.

"Yeah, we pulled him out of a pig farm south of Nibridge. He was housing the fugitive."

"What could a boy have done that we are going to this extent to find him? I heard he is only sixteen..."

Reigns smirked, "He must be something more than a sixteen-year-old. He nearly killed the Valkyn that was with us. Apparently, he shot him with some type of fire."

Ambros leaned in closer to Reigns, "Personally, I wish he would have finished him off. The way those Valkyns want us to worship the ground they walk on. Serves them right!"

Reigns's response was terse. "That's enough, Ambros. You will get us both executed for treason with that kind of talk."

Sighing, Ambros fastened Felix to the inside of the carriage. "You have to leave tomorrow, right? What are you going to do for the next few months?"

Reigns pondered the question. "I'll be going home to see my Elana and our little girl, Sophie. Then I'll work on the farm and get enough food for winter. We can barely scrape by on soldiering." In truth, Reigns had been looking forward to the following day for months, even dreaming of it on numerous cold nights.

"Alright. Well, I'm off to the capital. See you in a few months, Reigns."

The soldiers clasped hands with a slight nod and Ambros began driving the horses with a whip. In only a few minutes he was out of sight.

The next morning, Reigns, with a sack on his back and his sword on his side, started his trek home. He had often walked the busy road headed southwest toward the center of the empire. Now thirty years old, Reigns had spent much of his adult life marching in formation and patrolling the highways for robbers, which was an all-too-common problem. His home was in the Flat Plains where the empire harvested most of its food. Reigns had saved and bought a meager farm two years earlier and had yet to have a successful harvest. He dreamed of his farm becoming profitable so that he would be able to hang up his sword.

The way of the sword was not so easily given up for most men. It was one of the few viable ways to earn a consistent living within the empire. Most men, like Reigns, did it simply out of a need to provide for their family. Few men enjoyed collecting taxes, harassing citizens, and serving the empire. Reigns was a soldier not out of love for the empire but out of love for his family. It was the means by which he could reliably provide for them.

Reigns crested the top of the last hill from the mountainous lowlands and stared at the Flat Plains. The sky was orange and purple with a few clouds meandering along. The sight was breathtaking as the sun set over the smooth, cropped fields. The plains themselves were a patchwork quilt of different fields and farms. Reigns descended the hill. At the junction between mountain foothills and smooth plains was a small tavern called The Windy Sun. It was a staple of the road and was regularly, as it was this night, filled to bursting with patrons.

Reigns walked in through the door which had been propped open to let the cool evening air into the somewhat raucous tavern.

"Hello Horace!" Reigns called to a man standing behind the bar talking to another traveler.

The portly man ceased his conversation and walked over to Reigns. "Reigns, is that you? I hardly recognize you without the uniform."

"Do you happen to have a room available?"

"I do. Let me have the boy fetch your bags. I'm sorry to say but you missed supper. Though, if you want, we could heat something back up for you."

"That is quite alright, Horace. I ate on the road. What do I owe you for the room?" Reigns asked as he unshouldered his pack and handed it to one of the innkeeper's helpers.

"For one of the empire's bravest, nothing at all,"

he said with a cheeky smile.

"Horace, stop that. It is not right to be treated differently than the rest of these fine folks," Reigns said, motioning to the rest of the room. "I'm nothing better because I work for the empire."

"Fine, fine. You give me an hour of your time and buy a bottle of ale to split and we'll call it even."

"I'll take that offer, old friend. First, let me go clean the road dust off." Reigns could feel the dirt gritting between his toes as he spoke.

Horace nodded and said, "I'll expect you around nine, Reigns."

Reigns entered the modest room. The accommodations were quaint: a bed, a chair, a small wooden stand, and a pail of water with a rag. Reigns had been eager for this part of his journey home. Horace was an old friend who he had grown up terrorizing their town with as boys. Unfortunately it would not be good for business if it became common knowledge that he was good friends with a soldier. While no one would openly claim animosity toward the empire or the army, what they did behind closed doors and in taverns was a much different story. Dampening the rag, he wiped the layer of road dust from his body and hair. By the time he was finished cleaning, the once-clear bucket of water had become a mixture of dirt and grime.

After an hour passed and Reigns had recuperated from his travels, he went down the stairs to the main room. The room had a long bar stretching along one side and three long tables for patrons to sit, eat, and drink. On the opposite side of the room from the bar was a large fireplace with an enormous stone hearth that on cold nights would heat the room. Sitting by the hearth, tending the fire, was Horace. He sat in a red, wooden chair. Beside him, another chair sat empty, waiting for Reigns. Reigns turned to the bar and purchased the agreed-upon bottle of ale and two small tankards. With his payment in hand, he sat next to his boyhood friend.

"How is business, Horace?" Reigns asked, pouring the ale into the first tankard and handing it to Horace.

"Business has been fine. The soldiers and merchants keep me and the staff busy enough." Horace's eyes were distant as they stared into the fire.

"Then why do you look so sour? Are things going badly with Clarice?"

"No, no, no, it's just that I heard a rumor that—" he hushed his voice "—the empire—" he paused, "ransacked and killed a pig farmer named Felix. Do you know if that's true?" Horace looked at Reigns ready to study his response.

Quick on his feet, Reigns said, "I should not be discussing imperial business, Horace...but yes, the pig farmer and his property have been taken by the empire, but he was not killed." Reigns washed some bitterness out of his mouth by taking a sip of ale.

A look of disbelief, or disgust, flashed across Horace's face. "What could Felix have done? I mean, I have known the man for a number of years. He comes and stays here a few times a year, and he has always seemed sincere, maybe a little bit of a rascal, but to warrant his property being burned and prison?"

"He was not so innocent. He was harboring a fugitive of the empire." Reigns said, rather tersely but continued. "It would not be good for us to discuss the event further. You never know who might be watching." He glanced at the door and then each of the windows. Trying to change the subject, he issued a warning to his friend. "For that matter, if you are doing anything here with even a hint of illegality, I would recommend you stop. There has been a change in attitude from the top."

"You mean the fugitive boy?" Horace interrupted.

"The official position of the empire is that if you see any suspicious activity it is to be reported. For that matter, the empire's stance is that there is no fugitive boy."

"I saw the flyers they were carrying a few weeks ago, and you just said Felix was arrested for—"

Reigns grabbed Horace's arm and squeezed. Leaning in close, he whispered, "I have told you much because you are my friend, and for your own sake. Officially, there is no fugitive boy. But if you must know, the empire has been losing its collective mind trying to find this kid. He even took out a Valkyn."

"Pff! Good. Conceited creatures as they are," Horace said, between sips of ale.

"I can't reiterate enough how serious this is, Horace. No matter who asks, don't mention a fugitive boy. And last I heard of Felix, he wasn't being sent to prison; he was going to be interrogated by the emperor himself. In all my years I have never heard of such a thing. This kid is truly dangerous."

There was a pause as Horace seemed to digest the information. Then with a smile, he said, "How are Elana and Sophie? Sophie must be getting big."

The two carried on lighthearted conversation and

retired to bed at midnight.

As Reigns lay awake, trying to fall asleep, he went over the night at Felix's house. Reigns had not thought much about it at the time. In his mind he was just following orders, dealing with another criminal. Apparently, a highly dangerous one at that, but Horace vouching for Felix bothered him. Horace was an incredibly good judge of character and if he thought so highly of Felix.... What was so dangerous about a kid, a teenager... besides fireballs? Maybe Felix just took in a kid that he thought was lost and hungry, and Reigns had delivered him to his death for his kindness. *No, I was following orders. This kid is clearly dangerous to the empire. If he can fight a Valkyn, no one could stand up to him and Felix was an accomplice. Orders are orders are orders.* Reigns repeated the phrase until sleep finally found him.

Reigns woke up right before dawn as he always did. He repacked the few belonging he had removed from his pack and fastened his sword to the leather belt around his traveling tunic. As he departed, he made sure to see Horace and reiterate his warning about the empire's crackdown. With that, Reigns said goodbye to his friend and was off.

The next couple days of his journey took him through very different landscape than the first few. It was flatland as far as the eye could see, broken up only by tilled fields or cattle grazing. As Reigns walked, he noticed more and more farms had been boarded up than he had remembered. He knew the empire was making a bid to capitalize on the plains and further regulate the crops. Reigns, in fact, had purchased his farm agreeing to sell all excess crops to the empire which would feed their army and sell the remaining food to citizens. This contract had been offered to many of the farmers on the plains. Needless to say, if they didn't take it, they were sure to be out of business within a year. The empire used its prisoners and some hired hands to run the farms that it took outright. The number of burnt and abandoned buildings made Reigns feel slightly queasy.

Reigns journeyed across the plains for three days before arriving at the small town of Ragurni. His farm was about an hour's walk from the town. He stopped at the market to buy Sophie a candy and some flour for Elana. Back on track, he arrived at the small lane leading to his farm. He knelt and scooped the black soil into his hands and let it pour through the spaces between his fingers. He was home.

# 10

Sensing his own nakedness, Will slowly turned to face the soft but stern feminine voice. His jaw gawked awkwardly as he attempted to remain collected.

A young woman sat on one of the huge tree branches next to the river. Her eyes glowed green as much as his own glowed blue. She was tattooed but not to the extent that he was. She had a glowing green inscription on her left foot and more text on her right hand. The language was like nothing Will had ever seen. She was clothed in a crudely cut deer-hide garment that went from her shoulders to just above her knees.

His eyes were trained on her as he slowly inched toward his clothes. *Splash!* Will felt a hot flush of embarrassment rush through him as he tripped and fell into the cold water. He quickly stood up and struggled to gather his composure.

"Not very graceful are you, Angel?" the woman said with a slight hint of a joke.

"My name is Will. What is yours?" he managed to say, straining to get it out past his embarrassment.

"My name is Sihu," she responded.

Will reached his clothes on the branches and pulled his pants on faster than a blink of an eye.

The young woman jumped down and landed elegantly. The only sound as she landed was of the arrows knocking together in the quiver on her back. Their light clattering caused him to notice the bow in her left hand. As she drew closer, the flames of the fire showed that her skin tone was darker than most and that she was slender. Sihu's hair was dark black and had a few feathers in it. It was done into braid, which rested on her right shoulder.

Sihu spoke again. "What is your business in our forest, Angel?"

"My name is Will, not Angel," he said, desiring her to use it. "And I was being chased by the empire so I came here, knowing they are wary of this place."

She looked disappointedly at him. With judgmental eyes, she asked, "So Angel, you are a criminal? Well, we do not take criminals in our forest."

"I'm not a criminal! I don't even know why they are hunting me. I lived in Valkinridge, but I escaped. So I wouldn't say I'm a criminal, just a fugitive who has escaped a prison I didn't belong in." As Will answered, he realized that what he had hoped was going to be a pleasant conversation was actually an interrogation. Trying to change the tone, Will asked a question of his own. "Why are your eyes green?"

"You can see my eyes?" Sihu questioned, but continued without an answer from Will. "This is the mark of my people, much like I the blue is likely that of yours. Am I to presume the empire will pursue you into our forest?"

Will answered truthfully, "Yes, if they can."

Sihu continued her questioning. "Why should I not hand you over to them?"

Exacerbated, Will answered, "Please. My people have been imprisoned by the empire for hundreds of years. I seek to free them." The tone of his voice truly reflected the emotion of his heart.

"You are peculiar, Angel. Our chief will decide your fate."

*I don't like the sound of that.* "Why do you keep calling me Angel?"

"Because of your wings," Sihu answered, rather simply.

"What wings?"

She motioned for him to turn around. He did so.

Pointing at his back, she said, "There."

Will edged closer to the water and could see his reflection. He saw blue tattooed wings on his back. They started where the knives had cut him from the ceremony on his birthday. *Wings!* With that revelation, Will went into pensive thought. *Wings! I am a Valkyn. But I can't fly. These are just markings. What could they mean? I really need to get into the book from Felix.*

"I didn't know I had those," he said sheepishly.

"You are strange, Angel. We will be leaving at first light. I recommend you get your sleep. It will be a long trek."

"To where?" Will asked.

"To my village. All who enter our land must be judged." She strode over to where his pack was and took his sword.

"Hey! What are you doing?"

Will was indignant, but Sihu simply replied, "You

can have this back if the chief allows."

Annoyed, Will laid his pack out and lay down on the hide. Will stared at the stars and every once in a while, he looked over at Sihu. She was always watching, green eyes staring at him. Sihu was sitting up against one of the trees of the arc.

Finally, Will said, "Aren't you going to sleep?"

"I will sleep once I know my forest is safe from you. For that to happen we must see the chief."

Will rolled over and fell asleep.

Will dreamed the same dream again, but this time the king repeated, "Will, come to me. If you want to save your people, you must come to me."

It was not a request, but a command. Over and over, the dream continued. Will kept giving his reasons why he could not, but it never mattered.

When he woke up again, the sun was rising. He woke to a soreness that he never thought possible. His lower back felt as if it had been trampled upon by a horse. His shoulders throbbed at each individual incision given to him by the wolf. Will tried to get up, but he felt as if someone had tethered him to the ground. He commanded his muscles to do the tasks they were meant to do, but they only quivered slightly before giving up. Will rolled his head toward the fire and there sat Sihu.

Mysteriously, strength found him and he sat up with a slight groan.

Sihu had the fire going already and was cooking some freshly caught fish. When he saw her for the first time in the daylight his heart beat a little faster.

Will moseyed his way over to the fire and to be friendly asked, "How are you doing this morning?"

"Eat quickly. We must be on our way."

Will chose not to argue and ate the fish ravenously. He rolled up his pack and placed a few of his magic rocks in his pockets.

"Give those here," Sihu said, motioning to the rocks.

Will reluctantly handed his only weapons to Sihu. She merely crumbled them in her hand. Impressed, Will shouldered his pack. Sihu had no pack, but only her quiver with his sword now in it. She carried her bow in her left hand. Will noticed her tattoos did not disappear in the daylight as his did.

"Come, Angel." She led him into the forest off the beaten trails.

Sihu moved through the forest gracefully, as if she and the forest danced with one another. Leaves did not crackle under her feet. She avoided the sticks and branches that would not bear her weight if she stepped on them. Sihu did this all with elegance and without appearing awkward.

Will was not as graceful. When he wasn't hurried, he was quite good at keeping quiet, but it did not come naturally to him. As Will rushed, he crashed through the woody undergrowth, snapping sticks, rustling leaves, and breathing heavily in pursuit of Sihu.

As the two moved deeper and deeper into the forest, the trees loomed larger and larger. Will had never seen trees so big. No longer underground, various tree roots seemed to be all they walked on now. The roots Will walked along were the size of the fallen trees that he and his brother had once played on. The roots provided a clear walkway and bridges as needed. Sihu seemed content with the quiet. Will was not.

"How long have your people lived in this forest?" he inquired.

"My people originally came with the king when he tamed this land. We have no record of our time before that."

"So, you came with the Valkyns?" he asked.

"Yes, our people and the Valkyns came and settled as the king tamed the land. The humans came after," Sihu replied.

"Are there more tribes of your people?"

"We are all that remain. The empire killed all our people besides those remaining in this forest."

"How did you survive?"

"Initially we wanted nothing to do with war. The emperor said if we did not participate in the war we could live peaceably. The king told us that we were not obligated to fight, but he encouraged us to. Our people chose not to fight. Once the king and Valkyns surrendered, the empire snuck in under cover of darkness and razed our villages. Those who survived came to this forest and formed a resistance. We severely outmatched the empire in the forest. Many times, they have tried to invade and every time they incur heavy casualties. Eventually, they sued for peace, swearing never to step foot in our forest."

Will asked, "So your people have a truce with the empire?"

"Yes. For now."

This was slightly unsettling news. In an effort to keep things light, Will asked, "What do the inscriptions on your hand and foot mean? I have never seen that language."

Sihu answered, continuing to be a well of information, "It is the language of my people when we first arrived here. It is now known by very few even amongst our tribe. The inscription on my hand stands for hope. I am always reminded that no matter where I am or what the situation is, there is always hope."

"Why do you have such a reason to hope?" Will asked, only realizing after he spoke how cynical he sounded.

"Because I know that good will ultimately win. If I didn't believe that, there would be no point in life."

"What about the tattoo on your foot?" Will asked.

Sihu responded, "It is a name."

"Of someone important to you?" Will asked.

"Yes," she quipped.

"Who?"

She nonchalantly replied, "You don't need to know."

Feeling that he was making progress, Will tried to pull more information. "How old are you, Sihu?"

"I am seventeen."

"Wow, I just turned sixteen. Have you ever left this forest?"

"No, but someday I will. Unfortunately, part of our truce with the empire is that we will not venture beyond the Dark Forest's borders. It is almost as if we exist at their pleasure." Stopping abruptly, she pointed to a natural cove with a stream flowing through it.

Will had not even noticed how dark it had gotten. The place where they stopped was beautiful. On two sides were large moss-covered rocks and on the third side were massive roots.

"We will sleep here tonight and tomorrow you will see the chief."

Will did not argue. He untied his pack and rolled out his deer hide, grateful for the rest. He was still exhausted, his body still recovering from his wounds. His shoulder continually throbbed. He massaged the painful area gently. Although he tried not to, he visibly winced when he touched it.

"You are wounded?" Sihu inquired.

Will recounted the story of the wolf, embellishing just a bit to make himself seem tougher.

"Take your tunic off." She did not ask. He did so. She inspected his shoulders in the light of dusk.

"These are becoming infected. We need to deal with the infection before it spreads further." She pulled a small pouch out of her quiver, then reached down and unstrapped a beautiful dagger with a black blade and handle from its sheath on her ankle. "This will hurt," she said.

He looked into her eyes, now glowing noticeably green with the lack of sunlight. "I'm not scared of anything."

She smiled and replied, "I didn't say you were scared. I said it was going to hurt."

With a swift motion, she sliced open one of the pus-filled wounds. Pain shot from his shoulder to the surrounding area. He took a deep breath to keep from cursing or screaming. He didn't know which. Sihu continued and reopened each of the eight individual claw marks. She then went to the creek and emptied some crushed herbs from the pouch into her hand and added water until it was a paste. She applied the salve to the wounds. The paste created a warming sensation as it was applied to his raw wounds. After she was done, Sihu placed the small pouch and dagger back where they had come from and leaned against a rock while Will lay down on his humble bed and stared through the trees up at the stars.

"You were right," Will was the first to break the silence after a considerable time.

"Hmm?"

"That was incredibly painful. How did you learn to do that?"

"It is taught to all of our people. We are raised from birth to live in the forest and from the forest. That includes hunting, medicines, and many other things."

"Maybe someday you could come to the mountains and I will teach you something."

Sihu laughed.

"What?" Will said.

"When I leave the forest, I will not be going to some cold mountaintop."

"Where will you go then?"

She paused. "I have a destiny that I will fulfill, and the location is not the important thing."

# 11

Will and Sihu continued their march toward the village. There was another pause in the conversation and once again Will broke the silence.

"What is your chief like? What do you think he will do with me?"

"Our chief is a master warrior. He makes all decisions regarding intruders into the forest and those who break the law."

Will, growing concerned, asked, "And what happens to those he deems guilty of offenses?"

She looked as if a sudden realization had just hit her, "Please, no more talking. We have already interacted too much."

This change in emotion made Will push, "What happens, Sihu?"

"They are put to death...I am done speaking."

Taken aback, Will recognized her change as a way to protect herself. When he was young his father had given him a chicken to raise for slaughter, telling him not to get emotionally attached. Again and again, his father told him this, but Will got emotionally attached. And when the day came for slaughter, it crushed him. It was all he could do not to take the chicken and run away and save it from its fate. Now, Will was the chicken and it was becoming clear that Sihu thought she had gotten too close to a person destined for death.

That night the realization that he was likely going to die did not help Will fall asleep. Yet the same dream came again.

"Will, come to me. You must come to fulfill your purpose." the king said.

Will, with his own death heavy on his mind, replied cynically, "I *can't!* I'll be dead tomorrow!"

The king replied, "Will, come to me."

On and on it went. The tension was building in Will's chest.

"If I survive the meeting with the chief, I will come!"

In a flash, Will was out of the dream realm and back in reality. He was sitting up with his heart pounding. His hands were clenching his deer hide. He looked over and saw that Sihu was standing up staring at him. Her bow had an arrow nocked, pulled back, and directed at his chest. The two stayed like that, staring at each other.

Sihu spoke first. "Are you here, Angel?"

Confused, Will replied, "Where else would I be?"

She continued to question him. "Where were you?"

"I was right here. I was asleep." He started to move.

"Stay where you are!" Sihu shouted, tightening the grip on her weapon.

She looked different than before. Will was starting to get scared.

"What were you doing?"

"I was dreaming!"

Still holding his gaze, she said, "Yes, your body was here but where was your soul?"

Becoming a little irked, he responded, "In my body, while I slept..."

Sihu changed tactics. "Tell me about your dream."

Will recounted the dream to her. After hearing Will's account, and because the words he said that he had dreamed were the words he had been shouting into the forest matched, she said she believed him.

Dawn was creeping over the trees. Sihu reached for a piece of rope from Will's pack and cut it. Will crossed his legs and sat up. Her eyes were still trained on him. She came close.

"Hold your hands out." He did so and she tied his hands together.

"Is this really necessary?" Will complained.

"You left the forest under my watch. I believe I know where you went, but the chief would not be happy if I was lenient about this."

Will knew there was no point arguing with his captor.

Sihu tied his pack up and shouldered it herself.

"Let's move on."

On and on they went. The forest became a vast maze of roots, some towering over Will. The farther they went, the more they saw strange carving like the ones Will saw he first sprinted into the forest. As they rounded a grouping of roots, he saw smoke from a fire. In no time they were at the entrance to the village. It was an arch made of roots. They appeared to have been grown together, one braiding itself over the other. The entrance was alive with small leaves sprouting along the twisted roots.

They walked through the arch, an entryway to a series of large huts. They did not have straw roofs like the previous places he had been but were made from the hides of animals. On the hides were many drawings of what he presumed were battles and great hunts. Outside each tent, there was a small fire burning. Most had people cooking at them. All the people had the same dark skin tone as Sihu. Many of the women wore their hair in a braided style and wore similar garments as Sihu. All the men Will saw were shirtless, but what they lacked in a tunic they made up for in the massive tattoos covering their bodies. He saw one large structure in the middle of the village. The building was a long rectangular house with a roof made of sticks and moss. It had part of a tree incorporated into it, growing from it.

As Will looked around, all of the villagers' eyes were trained on him.

"Let's go," Sihu said.

She guided him directly to the large house in the center. On each side of the entrance was a warrior. One was female, the other male. Each was armed with a spear and had a black dagger strapped to their ankle. They each held their spear in a way that made Will recognize they were experts in using them. There was no running now. If he had planned on that, he should have done it in the nights preceding this moment.

Sihu spoke to them. "I have the Valkyn trespasser to see the chief. He should be expecting us."

*What? How is he expecting us? I have been with her*

*this whole time.*

"Yes, Sihu, he is. He has also convened the elders," the male guard said.

He pulled back the pelt covering the entrance.

Will and Sihu walked into a large room lit by a singular fire at the center. If the darkness hadn't made it difficult enough for Will to see, his eyes were now being assaulted by the smoke that filled the air. The smoke, oddly, was not from the fire but from a small congregation of men smoking pipes on the far side of the room. Sihu and Will made their way through the smoke and darkness to the group of men. As the two approached, the men each moved to a seat. They formed a crescent shape so that when Will and Sihu were close enough, they were surrounded on three sides. Sihu stopped and knelt. She elbowed Will in the thigh. He kneeled. As Will peeked out from under his bowed head, he was only able to make out the silhouettes of the men.

Someone in front of them stood up and slowly made his way toward them. His steps were out of rhythm. Will guessed he had a limp.

A man's gruff voice spoke. "Sihu, tell us all that has happened since you met this intruder."

She recounted the story of their meeting, even the part about Will falling in the water. He loathed that part. She included everything with great detail. As she spoke of his sleeping, she said, "He slept most nights muttering under his breath. It was mostly gibberish until last night. It was clear that he was speaking with someone. As I was observing him, he shot up in bed and his eyes burned bright blue and were open. He began to shout, saying that if he survived today, he would go to see this person."

The man standing said, "Thank you for your diligent service, Sihu. That will be all." She stood, bowed, and left the tent.

The man who Will presumed was the chief moved directly in front of him.

The man spoke calmly. "Look up, Will."

Will did so. As he did, someone threw a couple logs on the fire and the place was illuminated more brightly. He took in his surroundings. The inside of the long house was made of beams stripped of their bark. It appeared the bark had been used as the siding for the large building, with the smooth side facing in. Surrounding him were twelve elders, including the man currently standing in front of him. The elders sat cross-legged on mats. They were mostly gray-haired although two were not, nor was the man standing in front of him. All of the elders had worn looks to their faces. Will guessed most were in the final stages of life. Each of the elders smoked a pipe and gazed at him pensively.

"Will, do you know what happens to those who trespass in my tribe's forest?" the chief asked, calling Will's attention to his face.

He stared at the man who was in stark contrast to the rest. Will guessed this man was in his early forties, around his father's age. His tattoos were not black like all those he had seen thus far. His were white, almost as if they were the remains of healed wounds. The man had no shortage of the markings, either. This man looked more intimidating than anyone—or anything—Will had faced until this point in his journey, save perhaps the wolves.

"Well, Will?" he asked.

"They are executed for trespassing." Will

answered confidently but worried he would suffer the punishment.

"Correct. This forest is sacred to my people and you have desecrated it by entering it. The punishment for those who enter our forest is death. This rule has served us well and protected us from our enemies."

"Am I to be put to death?" Will asked, barely uttering the words.

"That depends how you answer this question. What is your purpose in life?"

Will's mind swirled, throwing suggested answers. *To be a good person. To join their tribe. I don't know!* And then it hit him.

"I believe it is my destiny to free the Valkyns held captive by the magic of the empire, and I currently seek to go to the imprisoned king."

Not revealing whether his answer was right or wrong, the chief asked, "You are a Valkyn, then?"

"Yes, I believe I am, though I have not flown and do not have physical wings. But it stands to reason that the village I come from is the last remnant of the Valkyn lineage who were not corrupted."

"Before we move forward, we must test your claim of being a Valkyn. I take no intruder at his word."

The elders simultaneously began to hum a low tone. *Hmmm.* Someone hit a drum—*boom!* Then another banged some sticks together. In rhythm, the hut filled with *hmmm-boom-tick, hmmm-boom-tick.* This went on for a short period of time creating a methodical cadence.

Suddenly the fire dimmed as if someone put a lid over it. In the darkness Will saw that the tattoos of those surrounding him were glowing green. Will's tattoos were now evident, and the chief's were still white, although now they were shining. The chief moved forward. His hand was in a fist but his thumb was up. The pad of his thumb glowed blue. The chief forcefully applied it to Will's forehead.

As soon as he touched Will, the wildness inside him burst through all his limbs. He felt a pain in both shoulder blades, as if someone had applied a hot iron. His initial reaction was to wince in pain but he did not move. He desired to see what was happening. He willed his eyes open and looked around. He saw blue wings on either side of him. They were coming from his back. They were his wings! He tried to move them, and they twitched slightly. They worked!

The chief removed his thumb, the elders stopped chanting, and the fire blazed again. As fast as it happened, his wings were gone. Will was left standing, just plain Will, once again.

# 12

"I am Chief White Lightning. It has been a long time since a Valkyn of Macceus has been in our forest, although we have seen and killed a few of Lushian's kind."

Relieved at the somewhat-kind introduction, Will responded, "I am pleased to meet you, Chief White Lightning."

The chief went on. "Last night, the king called to me. He told me that you would be coming through our village and that my people were to help you."

"Then why did you make me go through this whole interrogation?"

White Lightning smiled and replied, "Because moving and communicating through dreams can be easily misunderstood. I see now that you are the Valkyn the king spoke of and we will do everything in our power to help you get to him."

Thankful to know the chief's intentions, Will replied, "I thank you for your willingness to help."

"During your time with us, you will stay with Sihu's family since you have already become acquainted with her. The king informed me that you have no formal training in combat or reconnaissance, and he requested that we help you in those areas. If you agree to stay, our village will teach you these skills."

Will was excited for the opportunity to stay and learn more about how to defend himself from the creatures, beasts, and people that hunted him.

"I accept your offer!" Will said with excitement.

Just then a man burst into the room. "Chief, the empire sent a messenger. He is waiting at the entrance to the wood, and requires an audience with you."

The chief furrowed his brow. "What am I? Some slave to them? They call and I must answer them? What do they want?"

"He would not say. Only that he requires an audience with you."

"Tell him that you are my messenger as he is the empire's and that whatever he desires to say to me, he can say to you. I am not some dog to be ordered about."

The man bowed and left.

"Red Oak!" the chief called, his mood now turned sour.

The man who had been at the entrance came in. "Yes, Chief?" the guard answered.

"Take Will to Sihu. He is to stay with her family until he is ready to leave. That is all."

Will stood and bowed. He walked out of the tent following Red Oak. Breathing the fresh air was like breathing in new life, and he was grateful that his life was spared. The two weaved through the village of domed structures surrounded completely by a tall wall. It would not keep a serious enemy at bay, at least not for long.

As they turned a corner, he saw a familiar face. Sihu. His heart leapt. She was sitting beside a fire outside a domed hut. She did not see them yet. Her eyes were trained on the fire, looking into it as if desiring to escape the world. They got a little closer and Will saw a small stream running from the corner of her eye and down her nose. It formed a slow steady drip, which created a small pool of mud as it hit the ground. Will hated that she was crying.

They were only a few paces away when Will, as always, spoke first. "Are you alright, Sihu?"

She looked up. Her face lit with a smile, and in an instant, she hugged him.

As she embraced him, Red Oak cleared his throat.

Sihu immediately let go and gathered her composure. Will could have reached over and smacked Red Oak.

Red Oak said, "Sihu, the stranger is to stay with your family until he is ready to leave, by order of the chief," then turned and walked away.

Sihu gestured toward an old stump by the fire. "Sit and tell me what happened, Angel."

Will recounted to Sihu all that had happened. He was especially excited to talk about his wings and that the king visited both him and the chief. He ended with how he was to stay with her family until he was sufficiently trained in the sword and stealth.

Sihu listened intently to everything Will recounted. Once she was caught up to the current time, she said, "I must introduce you to my family."

She led him to the hut and pulled back the deer-hide curtain which served as the door. Will stepped in. The hut was just big enough to sleep about six people. It had a fire in the center, and a hole in the top of the ceiling allowing smoke to escape and light to come in. There were four mats laid out taking up most of one side of the small space. A number of weapons and tools, including bows and arrows, daggers, and a sword or two, leaned against the wall. Two people sat on the side opposite the mats.

They remained motionless, even at the interruption. The man had long, gray hair pulled back into a ponytail. He wore a tunic, unlike most of the men Will had seen in the village. Across from him was an older woman. She seemed younger than the man, with mostly black hair braided in two rows. She wore a garment similar to Sihu's. They sat cross-legged. The man held his hands out with palms facing toward the ceiling, and the woman's hands rested on his with her palms facing down.

Sihu and Will waited patiently for a few minutes for them to acknowledge their existence.

The man opened his eyes and looked toward them. "Sihu," he said with a raspy voice and a smile. "I am so glad you are home, and you brought a guest?"

Sihu explained the situation to her father.

He got up and stood in front of his guest, extending his hand. "Welcome, Will."

Will grasped the man's hand and bowed his head. "Thank you for accommodating me."

"Sihu, if Will is to learn how to be like our people, he must live like us. Come with me."

Sihu's father led them out of the tent to a small, grassy area beside their hut. "This is where you will make your dwelling."

Confused, Will looked from Sihu to her father a

couple times.

His confusion must have been evident, because Sihu's father spoke. "Sihu will instruct you on how to build your own hut. You are a man by most of our standards. It would not be appropriate for you to live in another man's house."

Will liked the challenge, but he was also weary from his journey.

"I would start sooner rather than later," Sihu's father said.

*I guess being a man is doing the important things even though you really want to do something else.*

Sihu ran into the hut and came out with an ax and a dagger. She handed the dagger to Will and said, "Since you are to be one us, this is for you. The blade is stone and will not go dull."

He strapped it to his ankle.

"The first thing you will need is posts," she said. "Follow me."

As Sihu led him through the village, Will asked her, "Why do they all stare?"

In a matter-of-fact tone, she replied, "Because you are the first outsider most of them have ever seen. As long as I have been alive you are the only stranger to come to the village and not be sentenced to death."

They passed through the tall wall through another braided archway.

Sihu and Will exited the village on a different side than they came in. A large field of maize immediately appeared in their view. Men and women were pulling ears off the stalks. It was a beautiful sight—the rows, and rows of corn. The biggest crop they had in the mountains were tubers.

Sihu and Will followed a beaten path around the fields. They entered the woods, now off the path, and hiked a brief distance to a grove of trees. The trees were tall and about the width of Will's forearm, only a few years old.

"We must select the ones that will not hurt the forest," she said, starting to inspect them.

"How do we know which ones those are?"

Sihu explained, "If they are growing so close together that you can't walk through them then only one of the two is going make it. We will take one, and one will live as it would naturally."

Eventually, they found three suitable trees and Will felled them. Tying them together, Sihu picked up the lighter front end and Will picked up the rear. The two made their way back to the village by the time the sun began to set.

"It looks like you will be sleeping under the stars tonight," Sihu said. Will undid his pack and threw his mat out.

"I like the stars," he said with a smile.

"You had better get some sleep," she said as she turned to enter the tent.

"Goodnight, Sihu," Will called out to her.

She turned and looked at him with a slight smile gracing her lips. "Goodnight, Angel." She then disappeared into the tent.

That night Will fell asleep easily. It was the first night he actually felt safe since he had turned sixteen. For the first time, Will was out of the empire's reach. Again, he had the dream where the king asked him to come.

This time, he replied, "I will be there soon."

Seeming satisfied with the answer, the king

allowed Will to move on to other dreams.

Will woke as the sun was cresting over the forest. The village seemed already alive though his host family was not awake. He went to where the fire had been the day before and rekindled it with some nearby sticks. By the time Sihu and her family emerged from the tent, the fire was hot enough to cook breakfast on. They cooked small cakes made from maize, topped with a berry paste.

After breakfast, Sihu informed Will that he was to attend the small school in the village. She walked him to a clearing near the edge of the village. To Will's embarrassment, most of the other pupils were no older than eleven or twelve.

Sihu said, "Wait here. Fox will be here shortly. Make your way back to our camp after you have finished the day's lesson."

"See you then..." Will grumbled.

A couple minutes after Sihu left, the portliest villager he had yet seen came to the school. The kids ran and tackled the large man, which quickly turned into wrestling.

After the children gave up hope, the man stood up and addressed Will. "You must be Will. My name is Fox and I will be giving you lessons in stealth."

*He doesn't look like much of a fox or very stealthy, but the villagers don't mess around.* "Glad to meet you, Fox. I am looking forward to the lesson."

Fox addressed the entire class as he said, "Follow me, children."

They followed Fox out of the gate and into the forest. As they walked along, the children kicked leaves and threw sticks and rocks at each other. In a quick motion, Fox abruptly stopped and held up his hand. The class then began to sneak quietly through the woods. Will was able to stay quiet and stealthy. He was proud of himself for being as quiet as the children. Then Fox made another stop and motioned Will to himself.

Once Will was close enough for him to hear, he pointed to a squirrel fifty paces away.

"Go and touch the squirrel."

*What?* Fox was not asking. *This is the lesson.* Will started slowly towards the squirrel. It had not seen the traveling class. Will avoided all the sticks on the ground. He took each step as if stepping on sharp rocks in bare feet. Will hid behind numerous trees until he was behind a tree about three paces away from the squirrel. Will stepped out and took the first of the final three steps. As his foot landed, the squirrel turned and looked directly at him. Will stood frozen. The squirrel inspected him and, in an instant, it took off. Will let out a huge pent-up breath and hung his head. The class was quickly behind him.

"That was much better than most people do on the first try, Will."

The words made him feel better until it was the small kid's turns. They were able to sneak up and touch chipmunks, squirrels, and even certain birds. Will did the math and he was the only one not to succeed. He waited and waited for his next opportunity, but by the time it would have been his turn again, they were back at camp.

The children quickly scattered. Will thanked Fox, assuring him that he would soon succeed. Will hated failure, especially when there was no opportunity for redemption. From that moment on, Will set about walking as silently as he could everywhere he went. He was not necessarily moving awkwardly or slowly, but he made conscious decisions to move through the village taking the quietest routes.

When he made it back to Sihu's family, dinner was being cooked. It was venison with a side of maize. It tasted sublime. After a diet of stew and dried meat, this meal was a revelation to his taste buds. Will had not had lunch and he got the feeling that lunch was not a normal meal for these people. After dinner, Sihu worked with Will to help him with his small hut.

First they stripped the bark off the trees they harvested the night before. To do this, they took a sharp dagger and cut a straight line lengthwise along the log. Sihu and Will worked from this seam and peeled the bark off in large sheets.

As they worked, Sihu gave Will pointers for sneaking up on animals. "Always approach from the opposite side of their food. They will be less likely to turn around."

The pair then dug holes for the posts. They used the family's campfire to dry out the recently stripped bark.

The sun had set so Sihu said, "Tomorrow we will lay the frame and attach the siding."

"Sounds good. Do you want to relax by the fire before bed?" Will asked.

Sihu gave a slight smile. "Sure."

As they sat there with light flickering across their faces, Will told her stories of his family and growing up in the mountains. Sihu was amazed at all the different customs, and she even asked him to go into great detail about the mountain.

"I have only ever known the forest," she lamented.

"Someday you will get out and see the world!" Will said confidently, trying to reassure his new friend.

When the moon was high, Sihu and Will said their goodnights and they were off to bed. As Will lay below the stars, he was grateful for the friend he had in Sihu.

# 13

After only a few weeks of being home, Reigns had his fields plowed and his first crops planted. The barley was just beginning to sprout as Reigns sat in the dirt with Sophie.

Sophie was singing a children's tune. "Run, run, run, spun, spun, spun, done, done, done." As she sang, she ran and spun and fell down.

As she lay in the dirt with mud on her face she looked up at Reigns, "Daddy, are you going to leave Mama and I again?"

He smiled as he looked down at the second greatest love of his life. "I don't want to go anywhere, sweetie."

"Good, because I don't want to you to ever leave me again!" she said resoundingly and in a blur, she was off again singing and spinning and falling.

That night after Sophie was in bed, Elana was doing dishes and Reigns was working on replacing the handle of the plow in their small barn.

*Clip-clop, clip-clop, clip- clop.* Reigns's ears perked, recognizing the hooves of an army runner. He peered out to see Ambros riding up the dirt lane, the horse kicking up dust clouds as it swiftly ran.

Reigns greeted him. "Ambros, what are you doing here?"

Ambros looked down. "I'm sorry Reigns, but the empire is calling you back to action. We are finally attacking the Forbidden Forest."

"The rebels? Don't we have a treaty with them?" Reigns said, almost incredulously.

Ambros lowered his voice. "We did, but apparently they are harboring the boy."

Reigns matched his hushed tone. "Why do they want this boy so badly?"

"I don't know, but if I were you I would report immediately. They are really cracking down even within the ranks. They are calling almost everyone off leave."

Reigns understood. Ambros was just the messenger. It would not do to take his rising anger out on his friend. Instead, he simply responded as a dutiful soldier. "Thanks for the heads up. Which barracks do I need to report to?"

Ambros handed Reigns's orders to him.

He unrolled the parchment and saw that it was the eastern barracks where he had just been stationed.

Just as fast as Ambros showed up, he was gone.

*Strange,* Reigns thought. *Ambros doesn't stop anywhere quickly. If anything he is usually disciplined for tardiness. Things really are changing.*

Reigns went inside and told Elana the news.

Tears streaked down her face, but then her anger flared. "You just got here! Whatever they want, they can do it without you!"

"El, I'm sorry. I want to be here, but if I don't go, they will throw me in the stocks or worse. Every day

I'm away from you and Sophie, I dream of being here with you two."

Elana sunk into his arms and wept. They sat in the silence with tears escaping late into the night. Reigns dreaded the conversation with Sophie he was going to have the next day.

Reigns woke just before sunrise and walked to the well to get the water for the day. As he walked through the plowed, soft soil, he pondered the strange dream he had the night before. In it, a king had called to him, but not just any king the Eternal King from the stories told around campfires and taverns. The king called him to go to Tizon and meet the boy named Will. Reigns tried to reason with the being, saying he had to report for duty, but it was impossible. The king would not see reason. Reigns pulled the bucket of fresh, clear water from the well. Strange dream, but it had been a rough night.

As Reigns crossed the threshold of the house, Sophie nearly tackled him as she embraced him. She still didn't know the news.

"Dada!" she screamed.

"Sophie," he replied smiling down at her.

After she released him, he asked, "Sophie would you like to go for a walk with me?"

"Oh, *yes!*"

"Alright, put your boots on and let's go."

The two walked down the rows of sprouting wheat and barley. The dirt seemed soft under their steps and created deep indentations as Reigns walked and Sophie skipped.

Once at the end of the rows Reigns knelt down and took Sophie's small hand in his large, calloused one. "Princess, I have some bad news."

Her face flushed with fear. "No, Dad..."

"The empire has called me back and I have to leave tomorrow..."

Sophie yanked her hand away and stuck up her nose.

The reaction tore something deep inside Reigns's chest.

"I hate the empire! I hate them! Don't go, Dada! Stay here. Don't leave me!"

"It's not my choice, sweetheart. I have to do it to take care of you and your mother."

Sophie raged, "The empire is *evil!* You shouldn't work for them."

Reigns grabbed her arm and drew her in close.

"Who taught you to say such things? Never say that again."

Sophie began to sob and fell into Reigns's chest. "I'm sorry, Dada. Don't leave me..."

"I'm sorry, Sophie. I don't want to."

Sophie pleaded and pleaded until she came to accept the fact that there was nothing she could do to make him stay. The two walked back to the house, but there was no skipping this time. Once in the house, Sophie ran into her room.

Elana looked at Reigns. "She was never going to take it well."

"I know," Reigns said, looking toward Sophie's bedroom.

"It's just because she loves you so much, Reigns."

"And you don't think I love her?"

"I didn't say that."

Reigns recognized that lashing out was uncalled for, and he felt even worse about himself.

"I'm sorry, Elana. It's just that I really thought I might be able to give up military service after this crop. And now, knowing what Sophie thinks of the empire, what does she think of me?"

"What does Sophie think of the empire?" Elana asked curiously.

"She shouted at me that they were evil. Do you have any idea where she could have heard that talk? She must think I am evil for working for them."

"You know she could have heard that from any of her friends' parents. The empire is not exactly a beloved institution. And as for you, she loves you and she hates that the empire takes you away. She has no grasp of whether it is good or bad. She just knows it takes her dada away from her."

Reigns stared at on knot on the wooden floor, processing the conversation they were having. He looked up at Elana, meeting her eyes, he asked, "Do you believe the empire is evil?"

There was an uncomfortable pause.

Eventually, Elana replied. "I think the empire provides us with a job and the means to make a living."

"That's not an answer to the question."

"I do not think they are good." She looked away as if she expected to be scolded for speaking ill of the empire.

Instead, Reigns spoke softly. "They are not good. I used to think they were because that is all I knew. But the more I learn, the more I wish I could un-know. I always believed it was good because without the empire and the army there would be chaos. I always trusted the high command, but after this last mission and now this summons, I just don't know."

Elana looked stunned. She probably never thought her warrior husband would doubt the high command of the empire.

"Just this one last mission, and then you will be up for retirement," she said softly. She strolled over and kissed him on the lips. "After this, no more. Even if it means we lose everything, you will not have to go back."

"If they summon me, even after I am retired, I must go back. They control us, Elana, we have no choice. We either serve or are branded as traitors."

"Just go on this last mission," Elana tried to encourage, "and maybe, just maybe we can have the life we have always wanted. Just dare to hope, Reigns. For me and for Sophie."

That night Reigns again had the strange dream of the Eternal King commanding him to head to Tizon to meet the boy the empire was searching for. Reigns awoke with a start in a cold sweat. And for the rest of the night, he altered between wakefulness and the same dream—now a nightmare that he could not shake. Giving up on sleep, he rose just before dawn and fetched the water for the day. This would be the last time he would draw the pail from his own well until he returned from his assignment.

The mood was somber as he walked through the wooden threshold. Elana had made cornmeal cakes for breakfast, packing some as traveling food. Sophie dragged her feet and walked to the door without looking at her father.

"I'll be back later," she said.

"Don't be too long. Your father has to leave at noon!" Elana called as Sophie trudged into the fields.

Reigns went about all the chores he could, trying to tie up loose ends so there would be less stress on Elana. As noon approached, Elana helped Reigns fit his pack with all the essentials.

As he was about to go search for Sophie, she strode in, walked to the corner of the room, and sat down. Reigns shouldered his pack and walked over to her.

"Sophie?" he said, but she did not look up.

"Sophie, look at me," he said sternly but also softly.

She turned her face up to him. He could see the trails of tears running down her face.

He attempted to comfort the four-year-old. "I love you, and I will be back. I'm not going to leave again. This is the last time."

Between sniffles Sophie asked, "You promise?"

"Yes, darling, I promise."

She reached in her pocket and pulled out a small, yellow flower—a weed to most but a beautiful flower to her.

"I got you this." She handed the flower with the broken and creased stem, damaged from her small pocket, to her father.

Reigns felt a tear slip from his eye and down his cheek as he scooped up his little girl and embraced her, never wanting to let her go though he knew he had to. He set her down and placed the flower in his tunic pocket.

Next he went over to Elana. The two had been in this position many times before. The summons came, and they must bid farewell. As they both took a moment to look into each other's eyes, they knew something was different this time. After that brief pause, Reigns kissed her and wrapped his arms around her. A few moments later, he released her, kissed her on the forehead, and said, "Goodbye Elana, I will think of you every day."

"And I you."

"And me!" Sophie chimed in.

With one last kiss to each of the most important people in his life, Reigns began the journey back to the barracks he had so recently left.

# 14

Over the following weeks, Will and Sihu finished the work on his small hut by attaching the dried-out bark as siding and using the hides of two deer as roofing. Will also became quite the animal stalker. He even managed to touch a bear. This was a milestone that allowed Will to move on to swordsmanship and archery in his training. He was already proficient with a bow from his hunting in the mountains. The sword, however, was a different story.

The person assigned to train him with the sword was not a friendly man like Fox. This man was simply known as Thunk. Will thought it an odd name and somewhat humorous when he heard it. But Thunk was not a man of humor or wit; he was always serious. Thunk was young but walked with a noticeable limp. He was more muscular than any man Will had ever seen. Each lesson started precisely at noon. One time Will was late and Thunk informed him there would be no lesson since he didn't care to show up on time. Will was always a few minutes early from then on.

For the first week of training, Thunk forced Will to learn the people's dances. They were graceful, but not dainty. No dance could look dainty with Thunk instructing. Once these were done, Thunk had Will hold a stick as he went through the motions of the dance, to work on the posture of his upper body.

Will worked with Thunk during the day and Sihu at night. They both constantly reminded Will that all fighting stemmed from footwork. These times led to drastic improvements in Will's ability to wield a sword. He quickly progressed through the various training stages and was allowed to duel. This was another time when Will had to show resilience. Most men would have given up after being knocked to the ground fifteen times, in addition to getting covered in bruises. Will was not just a man but a Valkyn, and he would complete the training assigned to him. He realized during these nightly contests how outmatched he would have been if he had fought Sihu when they first met.

Days in the village turned into weeks and then months. In two months, Will became proficient in stealth, archery, and the sword. Though he was proficient, he was no master, and continued training with Fox, Thunk, and Sihu. In addition, he had time to finally read *History of the Valkyns*. Will was able to gather so much from the small book.

He found information on the ritual that happened on his birthday. It had been going on for centuries and was the moment a Valkyn received his wings and true sight. He found that Valkyns' wings were not physical wings but were made up of a magical substance. According to the book, the wings could be willed into or out of existence, although Will had not been able to accomplish this. If worn too long, the book said, wings would become a permanent fixture of the Valkyn. For the most part, Valkyns had led a relatively jovial and happy existence. They celebrated many feasts and competed in games, especially games that consisted of flight.

In addition to learning the history of the Valkyns, Will studied the map diligently. Every time he opened it, he thought of Felix and remembered the cost that had been paid for him to escape with it. He rolled it out and tried to plot his next steps. He could see that between the Dark Forest and the mountain where the king was held prisoner, there was a great river, called the Grenvale, that flowed north. Along the river's eastern bank were two cities: Fizon, and Tizon, the capital.

Late one night, as Will was drifting off to sleep, a howl echoed in the distance. His blood turned cold. He bolted upright and out of his tent. Will's ears tingled, anticipating the shattering sound again, but there was none. *Sihu.* She was on patrol that night. Will thought he might have dreamed it. Convincing himself it was nothing, he crawled back into his hut but did not sleep.

He rose early and got the fire going then went to the gate to wait for the patrol to come back. There were a few other people gathered nearby.

"Did you hear the howl last night?" Will asked an old man with white hair.

"Yes, we have not heard a howl like that in many years. Since the truce was struck with empire, we have not had any wolves in these parts."

Will's heart sank.

The gates opened and, one by one, the scouts returned. Every scout was dragging a large, dead wolf or two. Eventually, Will saw Sihu. He ran up to her and gave her a hug.

"You're alright!" he exclaimed.

She looked deeply disturbed. She turned to Will almost with tears in her eyes. "All is not right. Evil has entered our forest."

"Sihu!" a stern voice said. It was the chief. He motioned for her to join the group of scouts gathered around him.

Will waited patiently for what seemed like an eternity until she was released from reporting. As he waited, he counted the gathered scouts. They were short five scouts from the normal patrol numbers.

Sihu approached Will. "We need to get back to our homes."

Without a moment to spare, she led him through the camp, dragging him by the arm as she rushed him through the village.

Once home, Sihu rounded on him. Grabbing him by the tunic, she pulled him close. She looked at him intently. There was something in her green eyes that Will hadn't seen before.

"Pack your things. You must leave."

He knew now the look in her eyes was fear.

"What? Why?"

"We were attacked by the empire's wolves. It was completely unexpected. They have not ventured into the Dark Forest since the treaty. The chief says you must leave. He does not desire to turn you over, but that means you can't be seen when their envoy comes for deliberation."

Will's chest began to tighten. He tried to swallow but his throat felt like something was lodged in it. He had sensed that he was become a part of this village. These people had become his own people but now he felt abandoned. He was the prey, and the predator was coming. Will did not blame the chief. He wanted these people, his friends, protected.

"I will be gone in a few minutes..."

As Will turned, Sihu released her grip and her hands fell limply to her sides.

Will walked swiftly to his small hut. *I thought I had more time here.* He ducked into the structure and began gathering his things. *It is for the best. If I stay any longer I will only bring suffering.* In a matter of moments, everything he owned was strapped to his back. As Will stood at the doorway, he pressed his forehead against one of the cool posts and took three deep breaths. The post made the hot blood coursing through him feel less intense. Taking one last deep breath, Will pulled the flap of his hut and stepped out.

# 15

Once the curtain was drawn, light assaulted Will's eyes. Looking around, he tried to blink the glare away. The village was moving chaotically, fearfully. Messengers were running here and there. Every man and woman carried a weapon of some sort. Sihu was no longer outside. Will could hear her speaking to her parents. He started to enter the hut but felt something tug on his heart. *It will be easier to just leave. Goodbyes have come too often and become too painful.* Dropping his outstretched hand to his side, Will turned and made his way toward the western gate.

Once through the gate, he continued westward using the sun as his guide. His emotions were strong, but with each step, he wrapped them into a small bundle and put them away. He had to keep his head and heart in check as he traveled. He could deal with his emotions later. For now, he had to retain his focus. He was heading for the Grenvale River. From there he would travel north through the twin cities of Fizon and Tizon.

He moved silently through the woods using his

newly honed skills. In his left hand, he held a bow. His right hand rested on the string holding the nocked arrow between his fingers, ready to fire if he encountered one of the wolves. As he crept silently, he heard some commotion ahead. He weighed whether to sneak around the sounds or to investigate. In a desire to help protect the village he had come to love, he stealthily stalked toward the sounds.

A gruff-sounding man shouted, "Move on, you filthy dogs!" Then a whip cracked.

Will climbed a tree. The small party began moving toward him. What he saw seemed strange. A group of two giant wolves and three men trudged through the woods. The wolves seemed hesitant and begrudging with every step. One man, presumably the one who had shouted, held a whip and was dressed, not in armor, but in a leather tunic. The other two were in full armor, holding swords and scanning the forest floor regularly. *Trained soldiers.*

As the party moved forward, Will assessed the best place to make his stand. Unfortunately, if he were to attack from the tree, he could not move and would easily be picked off. He decided it best to wait for them to pass underneath and then flank the group. Surprise was his greatest advantage with the numbers stacked against him. As the wolves drew near, Will realized that they may smell him, and indeed he could see a slight change in the one wolf's demeanor as it cocked its head at Will's scent on the forest floor. They were almost directly below him.

Just as the beast inhaled deeply, and Will surely thought he was caught, the man whipped the wolf and yelled, "Move along, hound. Find those forest dwellers!"

While the men moved under him, he heard their conversation.

"They say this forest is haunted," one soldier said.

The other responded, "I heard the people that live hear eat all those whose trespass."

*These men are not warriors, they are cowards. Thunk would teach them a lesson or two.* Though Will doubted their courage, he knew they would kill any of those he loved given the opportunity. They were now past his tree, and he began to silently climb down. Placing his feet firmly on two roots of the forest floor, he drew his arrow back. He placed the bigger wolf in his sights. He aimed right behind the beast's left shoulder, inhaled, and released the arrow.

The wolf let out a vicious howl as it thrashed before crashing to the ground. Will released the next arrow aimed at the second wolf, which missed the wolf's side but luckily hit it in the throat, ending it before it could take more than a step or two. The two soldiers looked back at Will. They quickly retrieved their bows from their backs. Will took this brief moment to take cover behind a nearby cluster of trees. The man with the whip rushed to his wolves while the soldiers took cover. After a few moments the soldiers began to slowly move toward where Will had been.

Will took aim at one of the soldiers. *Tink.* Will heard the arrow hit the soldier's chest and then saw him collapse. The other soldier, now knowing Will's whereabouts, released an arrow that struck the tree Will was hiding behind. He took off, trying to get to higher ground. *Crack!* Will felt the whip bite his ankle and he tumbled to the ground. In a moment, the soldier he once thought was cowardly was over him with his sword out. Will saw hate burning in his eyes. The soldier raised his sword and Will's heart quickened, the blood pulsing in his ears.

"You think a miserable pipsqueak like you can attack the empire's men?" he shouted. "I have news for you. We will burn this forest down! We will kill your people and we will—" The soldier began to choke, his sword dropped, and he reeled, stumbling like a drunkard. He fell right beside Will. There was an arrow lodged in his neck.

*Thunk.* Will followed the whip from his leg to the man's hand. The dirty man had dropped the whip and an arrow had appeared in his chest

"Will!"

He sat up.

"Will, are you okay?"

He followed the voice. Appearing almost out of thin air was Sihu.

"Sihu! What are you doing here?" Will said, excited to see her.

Sihu looked down, looking hurt. "You left me without saying goodbye."

Will looked at her, trying to catch her eyes, "Goodbyes seem to be too frequent, and saying goodbye to you and your family was going to be too hard. I...I just don't know if I could handle that."

She met his gaze and replied curtly, "Well you no longer need to fear goodbyes. I am coming with you."

"What?" Will exclaimed. "It is going to be too dangerous! We will be trying to sneak through the empire!"

"Clearly, you need someone with you," she said,

motioning to the carnage surrounding them.

Taking a moment to think through his options, Will responded, "I would be glad to have you on this quest with me."

In truth, he knew that Sihu could only help his cause, and he genuinely looked forward to having her along. The two continued without incident to the Grenvale River. Occasionally, they heard a far-off howl. Usually it sounded as though the beast was being put down. If there had been any bitterness between the two companions at the lack of farewell, it quickly evaporated, and they went back to their usual enjoyment of each other's company.

The Grenvale flowed north and was an incredibly wide river. Very few men had swam across or even possessed the strength to attempt the endeavor. Even if they could swim the vast expanse of moving water, there were many rapids and a swift current. Upon drinking in the sight, the two companions started north along the shore, continuing until they were a couple hundred paces from the edge of the forest.

# 16

The trip on the road through the Flat Plains was relatively uneventful, besides a persistent tide of heavy rain. It was during one of these storms at midday that Reigns spied the familiar sight of the Windy Sun Tavern in the distance. His mind immediately went to the cup of warm mead he would have with Horace, and the exchange of pleasant stories that they were sure to share in the coming night. As Reigns approached the building, he saw that the tavern was not as he had left it just a few weeks earlier. There was no sound coming from within, no firelight emitting from the windows, and most ominous, a number of windows were broken. Arriving at the small porch he, scraped the mud off his boots and onto the stairs out of habit. There was a board nailed across the door barring anyone from entering. Reigns, straining his muscles, pried the board off the door and cautiously ventured inside.

The scene was worse than he could have predicted. The tables were scattered and broken—not one stood upright. A number of chairs were shattered into splinters, evidently from being thrown across the room. The long bar where Horace had been rooted for decades still stood, but there were no gleaming bottles of spirits remaining. Whoever ransacked the inn seemed to have confiscated or drank the whole inventory. Reigns strode toward the bar, his steps sounding hollow as their sound echoed off the walls. He placed his hand on the bar and let the well-worn wood glide under his touch as he circled around behind the bar. He rounded the end and his heart lurched.

Where Reigns could only presume Horace had been during the fight, there now remained a grizzly smattering of blood. He could identify Horace's large crimson handprint on the cabinet door that led to a small pool of dried blood. From the pool, there were streak marks across the floor, as if Horace had been dragged from his position.

*Clip-clop, clip-clop.* Reigns heard the familiar sound of an army runner's horse outside the inn. He positioned himself at one of the broken windows and peered out. The rider looked familiar. It was the runner for the eastern barracks and his friend, Ambros.

Reigns stepped onto the porch and drew his hood back to reveal his face, trying not to startle the runner. "Ambros!" he shouted.

The rider heeled his horse, trotted it close to the inn, and cocked his head at Reigns. Ambros pulled his own hood back. "You nearly made me jump out of my skin, Reigns! You should know better than to surprise a runner." Ambros slid a miniature crossbow back into its pouch.

"If I didn't know it was you, Ambros, you would have never known I was here."

"Why are you creeping around old Horace's place anyway?"

"I was hoping to get a room for the night..."

"Look, Reigns, I know you were his friend, but he was in with the wrong people."

"You mean the army did this?" Reigns replied incredulously, his rising anger barely contained.

"He was dealing with the enemies of the empire. He wa—"

Reigns cut him off. "It looks like bandits ransacked the place. What happened to protocol? I find it hard to believe he wouldn't have shown up at the magistrate's had he been summoned."

Ambros's eyes glanced down and then away from Reigns. "There was no magisterial summons. The orders came straight from the emperor."

Reigns heart sunk.

"Reigns, as I said before, the empire is at war. Results, not protocol, are what the higher-ups are worried about. I should warn you, though, Horace is at the northeast barracks. The roads have been too wet to take a wagon out, but once things dry out, he'll be on the first one to Tizon." Ambros moved closer and looked Reigns in the eyes. "Please, Reigns, just stay away from him. If anyone finds out that you two are close, there is no telling what the empire might do to you or your family."

At the mention of the potential threat to his family, a vein in Reigns's neck began to pulse.

It must have been visible to Ambros because he quickly said, "I had best be going. No time for catching up." And in a flash, he turned the horse and was off.

On the porch, Reigns leaned his back against the

wall of the inn. His cool, wet cloak sent a shiver through his body. After a few moments of contemplation, his mind was made up. He no longer trusted the leaders in the military. They had squandered all respect he had for them when he saw the way the missions to capture Felix and Horace had been completed. He had invested sweat and blood into the army. He had fought for the good of the people. But now to serve the empire, to serve the emperor, was to commit egregious offenses to the people of the land he was to protect. *I won't stand by as they terrorize their own people anymore. I have to save Horace.*

Reigns approached the barracks entrance. A small man stood guard at the western gate. Everyone knew Reigns at the barracks, but as he got closer, he didn't recognize this man.

"Name?" the man inquired.

"Reigns of the eastern troop."

The man pulled some parchment from his back pocket. Reigns watched his eyes cascade down the list of names.

"Ah, yes sir, Reigns. We have been expecting you. Please report to Captain Dration."

"Who?"

"Captain Dration. He arrived from the capital yesterday, sir. I believe you best hurry. Rumor has it we will be on the march to the Dark Forest on the morrow."

"Thanks," Reigns gestured to the man.

"My name is Rogen, sir."

"Thank you, Rogen."

Reigns moved through the barracks with speed,

using the knowledge he had acquired from spending years stationed there. He quickly made his way to the barrack prison. It was a small, wooden building with a thatched roof, guarded by two soldiers—two friends. Reigns weighed the option of gaining access by entering under false orders, but he knew that it would only cause his friends to be punished for oversight. Instead, he had to take the path of greater risk to himself. He had to incapacitate them.

Reigns busied himself with sharpening and oiling his sword until a few hours after midnight when the soldiers' awareness would be least vigilant. Wrapped in his black traveling cloak, Reigns scaled an unprotected wall. Positioning himself above the soldiers, he dropped down quickly, knocking one out with a small wooden table leg that he had snapped off the end table of an unsuspecting officer's quarters. The second soldier blocked Reigns's strike. The soldier raised his sword and a look of shock swept across his face.

"Reigns?" he gasped in disbelief.

This brief moment allowed Reigns to knock the sword and deliver a swift blow, knocking the man unconscious. Reigns dragged the men into the shadows after ensuring they were both not seriously injured. He then walked confidently into the barracks prison.

Horace was on a cot in the cell immediately to the right. Wasting no time, Reigns walked over to the secret hiding place of the back-up key and unlocked Horace's cell. Horace seemed to be asleep. Reigns shook the snoring man.

"What? Get off—!"

Reigns covered his mouth before Horace had the

whole barracks swarming like ants.

"Horace, I'm here to break you out!" Reigns hissed.

"Reigns, don't. They'll kill you... they'll kill your girls."

"You're going to make sure that doesn't happen." Reigns said in a matter-of-fact tone.

Reigns unlocked Horace's cuffs.

"Reigns, it's not worth it! I've seen how far they are willing to go..." Horace had tears in his eyes as he looked to his friend.

"They killed her, Reigns. They killed Clarice. I— I tried to stop them." Horace rubbed at the nubs that had once been his index and middle finger on his left hand.

Reigns never thought they would allow the killing of civilians. "That makes getting you out of here quickly all the more important. I'll explain later. Just trust me."

Reigns snuck Horace through the camp. He knew the guards' rotations like the back of his own hand. They made their way to the stables. There was only a runner's horse. Reigns saddled the beast, which was built for speed. The saddle and tack were all extremely light in order to increase speed and distance. Once saddled, Reigns used his club to incapacitate Rogen.

As soon as the two were in the cover of the closest wood line, Reigns dismounted and grabbed the bridle then looked Horace earnestly in the eyes.

"Horace, don't look down, look at me and pay attention. Big things are happening. Whether you wanted to be involved in it or not, you are, and for that matter, so am I. Any minute the patrols will find one of the bodies we left behind and will know that I helped you escape, which means they will go after Elana and Sophie. I need you to take this horse and go to them. Take them to the old ruins by Kadesh. Do you remember our adventures as kids and the hidden passages at Kadesh?"

Horace nodded.

"Good. Take them there and keep them safe. I will send word as soon as I am able. All I can say now is that I am following the direction of the Eternal King."

Horace's expression changed slightly, as though he had a million questions, but Reigns held up his hand.

"I don't have time to explain everything. Give Elana this and she will know that I sent you."

Reigns handed Horace the small weed flower that Sophie gave him. He had kept the flower in a folded piece of paper in his pocket. Just then a bell rang from the barracks. The two embraced, clasping each other on the back.

"Speed to you brother," Reigns said.

Horace replied, "And stealth to you, brother."

With that, Horace drove the horse down the road and Reigns slipped into the shadows.

# 17

Once Sihu and Will saw the vast, rolling prairie between the trees of the forest's wood line, they slowed down. Sihu motioned to Will to remain where he was while she scouted ahead. Will's pride was slightly hurt. A woman he cared for was putting herself in harm's way while he stayed back. *If we are going to survive this journey, we must play to each other's strengths, and she is the better scout.* Will repeated the reasoning continuously until Sihu's return.

"I saw countless fires far to the east. It must be the army. The men we encountered must have been a scouting party looking for the village," Sihu reported.

Will took the lead. "We better keep moving. Darkness is going to be our friend once we are out of the woods. That is, unless there is a Valkyn after us."

"I believe my people will give us some time to get out, at least tonight. Plus, if there is a Valkyn, besides you," she winked at him, "he will be just as easily visible to us."

Will twirled the magic stones in his pocket,

thinking of the last Valkyn he battled. "Let's move out."

The two moved seamlessly through the night. From then on, they traveled by day. They snuck noiselessly along the bank of the great river throughout the day, then at night they wrapped some sticks in leather and practiced their swordsmanship. The wrap was essential to reduce noise, but Will did not complain that it also resulted in fewer bruises. They traveled on like this for six days. As the seventh night approached, something caught Will's eye.

"Look!" Will pointed into the distance. There on top of a large hill, not quite like the mountains Will grew up on, something was on fire. It looked as if the whole hilltop was consumed in flames. It was particularly obvious since it must have been the only hill for leagues, and the bright orange-and-red flames contrasted with the vast expanse of darkness that was the sky. It looked like a giant bonfire.

"What do you think that is?" Will asked Sihu.

She unfurled the map, ran a finger along the bends in the river, and said, "We are almost to Fizon. It must be part of the city."

When the sun peaked up over the trees, and the mist rose from Grenvale, the duo started to move in the direction of the lonely hill that had been ablaze in the night. As they drew closer, they crossed over well-worn clay roads.

When the city came into view, both travelers were stunned. Fizon had the appearance of an inverted funnel. Neither had seen such engineering from man, Will being from his small mountain village and Sihu from her isolated forest. The first thing they noticed was that the hill was actually in the middle of the city and on top was a grand temple. The city was divided into three sections: the hill with the temple, the area surrounding the hill which was made of taller, well-kept buildings, and a vast hodgepodge of buildings of differing sizes and styles. There was a giant stone wall surrounding the entire city.

Will and Sihu continued toward Fizon, taking note of the city's details. There was a large gate and portcullis on the side they were approaching. There appeared to be an even larger gate toward the Grenvale River. There on the Grenvale was a massive system of docks, with workers running like ants in every direction. They could not see much to the east nor anything to the north.

As people passed along the paths and roads, the two travelers hid out of sight and studied the citizens of the empire. Neither had ever seen people dressed so strangely or fashionably. Some men were dressed in lightweight, flamboyantly colored garments. Other men were dressed similar to Will, obviously impoverished compared to the others. The seemingly wealthier women wore large, puffy dresses. Sihu was aghast at how a woman could wear such impractical clothing. Those of the lower class wore slim-fitting, and what appeared to be hand-me-down, dresses made from leather or cotton. Both classes of women had powdered-white faces with dark lines outlining their eyes. Will realized that they were not going to get far with Sihu wearing her traditional forest garb and her dark skin being especially evident. Sihu acknowledged Will's concern with a head nod.

When a solo woman traveler came along, Sihu slipped off after her. A few moments later, Sihu emerged dressed in typical lower-class fashion. She was carrying a small pouch.

"What's in the pouch?" Will asked.

Sihu looked at him with a slightly disgusted look. "Face powder," she spat.

She sat down and removed a small brush from the pouch and began to powder her face. Not long after, she looked at Will with her green eyes from behind a pale mask.

Will disliked the new look. He preferred her as she was. His opinion didn't matter, though; the goal was to go unnoticed.

Next, Sihu pulled a piece of something that looked like coal out of the pouch and traced her eyes.

"No one will be able to tell we don't belong!" Will said, hoping his enthusiasm would rub off on Sihu.

She grimaced at him.

The two took the road toward the city and rehearsed their back-story. They were a brother and sister traveling to the city to buy flour for their family. Their names would be Michelle and Tion and their family owned a beef farm. They were from the southwest just outside of the Dark Forest.

Guards stood outside the entrance gate, taking down names and purposes of all those who entered Fizon. As Sihu and Will approached, the sheer grandeur of the city began to overwhelm them.

"Boy!" the guard called.

Will hadn't realized it was his turn. "S-Sorry sir, this is my first time to the city," he said, truthfully.

The guard eyed him suspiciously. "Name and

business?"

"My sister, Michelle, and myself, Tion, are here to get flour for our family."

After another quizzical look, the guard changed his demeanor.

"Alright, boy, don't cause no trouble for us, and for the sakes of you and your sister, stay out of the red district. Next!"

It was nearly impossible not to let their eyes wander along the strange structures and buildings. When they were able to rectify their focus back onto their immediate surroundings, they noticed the city was grand, but it was also dirty. The streets had gutters filled with waste. Debris was scattered over everything, from old wash buckets to foul-smelling rags. The smell of the city was so assaulting that Will would have preferred Felix's pigs. The people were rude and rushed, constantly pushing to get through busy intersections.

"We should find a place to stay the night," Sihu said.

Will gave her a nod in agreement. After a few more minutes of wandering, they saw a place called Myron's Inn. It advertised a room and meal for three pieces of silver, which from what the other inns were advertising, was slightly pricey, but it was in the area that did not smell as bad as the others. Will and Sihu decided it was as good a place as any and went in. Sihu stood slightly behind Will as he approached the bar to talk to the innkeeper.

"I would like a room for myself and my sister," Will said.

"Sure, sure, my boy. That will be four silvers. Three for the room and meal and an additional one for the meal of your sister," the innkeeper said, repeating the words as if for the millionth time.

"Fair is fair," Will said.

Will opened his meager coin purse and paid the man. The man called to a young boy who Will had not seen.

"Finn, lead these two to room fourteen."

Finn approached and said, "Follow me if ya will."

Sihu and Will followed the boy up two flights of stairs and down a narrow hallway lined with doors. He stopped at a door with the number fourteen carved into it.

"Here ya are, sir and miss." He held out his hand.

Will knew what he wanted. *A tip? For showing us to our rooms. Seriously?* Will knew a confrontation would only lead to suspicion and he reached in his purse and pulled out a small bronze and placed it in the boy's hand.

"Thank ya!" Finn said, a little too chipper. And he was off.

The room left much to be desired. It had one small bed, a chair, a small table, and a window that looked down onto the busy street.

"I'll take the floor," Will said as he shucked off his pack and laid it on the mostly clean, wooden floor.

Sihu looked as though she was going to argue the point but decided to concede. She gave Will a smile and said, "Thank you, I appreciate your thoughtfulness."

Will felt his face blush. He joked, "Plus, I don't think you could handle sleeping on such a hard floor."

He gave it a few knocks to emphasize the

hardness. With that, Sihu elbowed him in the ribs and they both laughed. It was the first time they really laughed together since they left the village.

The laughter seemed to break a façade that they were both trying to hold. They, after all, were still just sixteen and seventeen, respectively. That night they were able to talk and tell stories about growing up. It was just like the fireside chats they had in the village. As the two lay in their separate beds, they began to fade into sleep. Although, every time there was a silence, one of them would try to fill with a new story, not wanting the night to end. In the morning they would have to resume their mission, but for a brief time, they were able to be kids again.

The morning came and the two packed up their belongings, in case they needed to make a quick exit from the city, and headed down to the common room. Breakfast was eggs and porridge. Will grabbed a table by the window as the server brought over two plates and cups of water.

"We need supplies and then we should get out of here," Will said right off the bat.

"We should also find out what we can about the army attacking the forest. They must have come through here. I want to know how my people are holding up."

"I will get our supplies and secure passage on a ship. You see what information you can turn up on the army and—"

Before Will could continue, the shine on the top of someone's head walking by caught his attention. It looked like someone familiar. The man was short and large, but before Will could place him, the man disappeared into the crowd.

"What is it?" Sihu asked, sounding slightly alarmed.

"Nothing. I just thought I saw someone I might know."

"How would you know anyone in Fizon? We are the only people each other knows outside of the forest."

Will let it drop and they continued with their plans.

They decided they would draw less attention if they split up, starting at the inn. Before departing, though, they decided to spend one more night at the inn and book passage to the capital first thing in the morning. They would rendezvous at the temple atop the lone hill near sunset. When Sihu tried to refer to it as a mountain, Will would not hear of it. She did not argue, and off they went.

Will made his way toward the docks. It was difficult to navigate his way there, but he followed the smell of the fish market. Once he found the source of the odor, he almost vomited. Fish heads and guts were piled and rotting. Right next to the piles of fish offal, tables were lined with filleted fish, perhaps fresh or perhaps not. Either way, they were being sold. Flies swarmed everywhere, landing between the guts and the heads and the fish for sale. As Will moved toward the great river, he took note that the innkeeper from his inn was there buying fish, causing his stomach to churn as he remembered last night's dinner.

There were a number of companies advertising travel fare. Will chose the one that looked the least likely to murder him in his sleep. He approached the small hut where an older man with a long, white beard and a sailor's cap was sitting.

"I would like to book passage to Tizon."

The old man, without saying a word, looked Will up and down. After what seemed like tens of minutes, he said, "Would ye noe? What'r business does'n a boy such as yerself have in the capital?"

"It's personal," Will responded, hoping the man would just let the question slide.

"Well, that won' do, sonny. Ye see, I hafts to have me manifest in order, an' personal business won' appease our overlords. So, what be yer business?"

"My sister and I are going to visit family in the capital. Is that good enough?"

"Yes, yes, that wi do fer me, but ye might hav issue with the guards at the city wharf. Ye will be payin now, then."

It was not a question. Will forked over the few silvers and received two boarding slips from the old man.

Will went to the market to stock up on a few supplies, primarily dried and salted foods that would travel well and provide optimum energy. He picked up a few herbs that Sihu requested from the spice market. As Will wandered through the markets, a shimmer of green caught his eye. It was a necklace in a bin with a plethora of other trinkets. The necklace had a roughly hewn green gem that looked like the same color as Sihu's eyes. It was attached to a bronze chain.

The man behind the booth homed in on Will's interest.

"You like it? It is one of a kind, nothing like it exists anywhere else in the empire. I will give you a special price if you buy it right now! Thirty silvers."

*Thirty silvers! What a crook! I don't even know if Sihu likes this kind of stuff. She might be upset with me for spending money on it.*

Will turned to the man, "What do I look like, a prince? I have never even seen thirty silvers!"

The peddler responded, "No, you are right, but because I can see you really want it, I will do you a favor. Fifteen silvers."

*What a crook to drop down that much.*

Will inspected the piece further. "This is a bronze chain and the gemstone is not that rare. I will give you five silvers."

The man scoffed. "Five silvers? Listen here, boy, I have a family to feed. This," he held up the necklace, "is for a woman you love, no?"

Will blushed at the assertion and the man must have seen it.

"I will sell it to you for ten silvers. Final price."

Will knew his blushing had cost him a cheaper price. "Eight silvers."

"Ten is the lowest I will take. If you don't want it, you can leave," the man replied.

Will forked over the ten silvers and placed the necklace in his pocket. *Dumb, dumb, dumb! Why did I do that? When am I even supposed to give this to her?*

# 18

The rain fell unrelentingly since the night Reigns broke Horace out of the northeast barracks. The constant washing of fresh mud over the road only aided Reigns in avoiding capture. He initially ran from the barracks as fast and as long as he could. After this initial burst, he opted for a more methodical approach. With the heavy rains, neither beast nor man could follow his tracks or scent. Reigns stuck to sneaking parallel to the roads that he knew so well from his patrols as a soldier. He quickly realized that despite spending a large portion of his military career in the area, he had never ventured far into the wild. His comfort was with what he knew and that was the road.

Reigns decided that it would be best to avoid the most direct roads to reach Tizon and instead take a slightly more circular route. This might throw off anyone pursuing him, but it meant that he would have to pass through the city of Petronev.

Petronev lay at the base of the Northern Mountains. It was called The Crimson City, not for the actual color of the city, but because blood flowed through its streets.

Petronev was renowned for gangs, bandits, and death. Stories of men and women who went into the city but never came out were regularly told at inns. Reigns had never traveled there, but he knew a few soldiers who were products of the city. They were the type of men who showed no remorse or cares when they killed. Killing was not their last resort but often their first.

Reigns often wondered why the army did not upturn the city and remove the blight from the empire. The only legitimate excuse, among many rumors and theories, was that the emperor himself oversaw the government of the city, and that he received a portion of the dirty money. The city even had spectacles in which those who were arrested were forced to fight to the death. Everyone knew the participants were not actual criminals, but merely rounded up by the city guard as the "games" drew near. The thought of Petronev and its corruption left a sour taste in Reigns's mouth.

Reigns continued to travel just out of sight of the road. The course was slow due to constant climbing over, going under, and walking around fallen trees and brush. His most difficult challenge was to stay warm at night. His first night and day in the rain was easy. His well-waxed traveling cloak had kept the water from soaking his clothes underneath. Unfortunately, as he walked through tall grasses and brush, the water on these plants broke through the protective layer. By the second night, when he first dared to rest for a few hours, he was cold and wet. He never reached a deep sleep. On the third night, he found a small fir tree that was mostly shielded from the rain. Reigns draped his cloak above himself to ensure complete dryness and stripped off a layer of wet, cold clothing. He hung the wet clothes in a few branches, hoping the slight breeze would dry them. Sitting on some dry needles with his back against the trunk, he dozed off.

When he woke, the area around him was only slightly lighter. He peered through the branches at the dark rain clouds and realized he was in for another day of wet travel. Placing his clothes back on he was disconcerted to realize that they had not dried in the least. He fastened his cloak and made for the road to get his bearings.

Once in sight of the road, he recognized a small, long-abandoned watchtower with smoke coming from somewhere within. *No one has been in there since the Great War.* Reigns was not naturally a curious person, but this was too strange. He had been part of a unit that cleared squatters from such places. Though abandoned, it was still empire property, and the empire did not permit trespassing. Stranger still, a military unit passed by this tower at least once every two days. He wondered who would be so bold as to risk an encounter with a detachment of the empire's soldiers. Reigns decided that it was worth the risk of an encounter if he could potentially find a powerful ally. But he was also conscious of the ever-present threat of bandits.

Reigns crept toward the old, worn tower. As Reigns approached, he took in the sight. It was only two-and-a-half stories tall. It had once been higher, judging by the amount of rough-cut stone on the ground around it. The upper levels had been toppled long ago. There was a doorway where a wooden door had once hung, but time had rotted the wood, leaving only the hinges. There were a few windows, but they were filled in crudely with rock from the surrounding ground. Reigns approached cautiously. He crept along the base of the tower until he was almost to the door. He then heard a sharp crack followed by a terrible shriek.

"I told you to be quiet!" a vile-sounding voice said.

*Crack!* Again, the unmistakable sound of a whip.

A woman's voice shrieked.

"Let that be a lesson to the rest of yous."

Reigns did not recognize the accent of the man.

"Take it easy, Chak. Yi don't want to be damaging the merchandise."

"Shut up, Slink. We'll be lucky if we get anything for this lot."

"Still, if they can fight, the guard at Ptronev will take'm."

*Slavers.* Reigns gritted his teeth and slowly drew his sword from its scabbard.

"I gotta take a leak. Will that stew be ready when I get beck?"

"It wouldn't take so long, Chak, if you didn't bring wet wood. Look at this smoke!"

Chak grunted, and Reigns heard footsteps coming from the hazy corridor. Chak did not take a second step out the doorway before a swift slash from Reigns's blade ended him. Reigns guided the slaver's body to the ground, not letting it make a sound.

Reigns entered the smoky corridor. Each step was measured. He took care not to kick any dislodged rocks or other debris. He moved like a phantom through the smoky fog. After a few moments, Reigns encountered the room that was the source of smoke and flickering light. In the center was the fire. Directly across the fire from Reigns, a man stood over a small pot. To either side were the silhouettes of people, motionless. Reigns picked up a heavy rock and threw it, striking the man.

"What the heck, Chak! I oughtta—"

The last words did not leave his mouth before Reigns closed the distance and dispatched him.

Reigns rounded and faced the rest of the room, just in case he had missed someone. No one moved a muscle. They all just stared. Reigns could make out hollow, starved faces in the firelight. They stared hauntingly at him, like the faces of the dead. After a few moments, Reigns bent down and wiped his blade on the deceased man's tunic, then sheathed the deadly weapon. Reigns walked closer to the fire and stoked it with what wood was left. The room illuminated brightly.

Reigns was horrified. A woman lay close to him. Red, bloody lines streaked her face. Near her, a young boy, no more than eleven, held her hand. Circling the room, he saw numerous women, boys, and girls. There was not a fully-grown man among them. They had all been badly neglected, and Reigns judged that most were on the brink of death. It was clear that the whip had visited each of them. The slavers apparently had no restraint. Lines, some red, some black-and-blue, marked faces, arms, and legs. The people's clothes bore marks of being ripped through by the atrocious weapon. Reigns picked up the whip near his feet and threw it into the fire. This action seemed to break the people from their trance.

Reigns took count. There were four women and seven children of varying ages.

"We need to get you out of here and away from this place," Reigns said.

The captives seemed to start making sense of what had just happened and sat up.

Reigns continued, "There is some stew here, eat of it what you can, but you have to leave as soon as possible."

A woman spoke up, "Where will we go?"

"Go back to your families if you have them."

The woman replied, "These men," she motioned to the corpse, "killed our husbands. We have no one."

Reigns racked his brain. *I can't take them with me. But where can I send them?*

"I know a place we could hide," the young boy who was holding the woman's hand spoke. "There is a marsh not far from here. It is haunted, so no one goes there. We might be able to live there."

Reigns jumped at the suggestion.

"Do you think you could guide everyone there?"

"We only got taken a couple days ago, and...well... my pop...he used to hunt near there. He took me a couple times."

"Alright. Take whatever you can and make your way there. If you have any extended family, go to them. The other slaver is dead outside."

"You're leaving us?" the outspoken woman said, aghast.

"I do not want to, but I have a mission I must complete, and it is taking me to Petronev. I wouldn't dare to have you accompany me there. What is the name of the Marsh? I will send help as soon as I can."

"It is called the Valley of Tears," the boy muttered.

Reigns did not want to prolong the process, so he barked orders here and there and got all of the captives up and moving. He had to be strong for them. If they sensed uncertainty in him, they would not trust him. As they left, Reigns pulled the boy aside.

"What's your name, boy?"

"Atslan"

"Listen, Atslan. I know you have had the worst days of your life here. I'm not going to candy coat anything. You have a tough road ahead. Stay off the main road and get these people to safety. You have to lead, and you have to be strong. If anyone comes to you, ask him or her who sends them. If they reply anything but 'Sophia's Rose,' they are not to be trusted. Do you understand me?"

"Yes, Sir! I do. I will try not to let you down."

"You won't, Atslan. Be strong."

# 19

Reigns traveled as quickly as possible the rest of the day. He pushed thoughts of the gaunt captives from his mind, choosing instead to focus on the most efficient route through the undergrowth.

That night the rain finally broke. Reigns still did not dare to build a fire, but once again found a dry spot under a fir tree to sleep. After draping the wettest of his clothes on the branches, he lay down and closed his eyes.

Reigns's dreams became night terrors. In one dream, he was in Petronev and the city guard captured him. When he went to compete in the games, he had to fight Atslan. The emperor was there. When Reigns refused, the emperor sent an army of the half-starved slaves to attack him. They surrounded him and impaled him with spears. Reigns woke in a cold sweat. Until this dream, he did not realize how evil the emperor was. The emperor was a patron and facilitator as women and children fought each other to the death. Sleep would not find Reigns the rest of the night.

Taking advantage of his inability to sleep, Reigns

got an earlier start than he otherwise would have. The storm yielded to sunshine, with only a few light clouds drifting lazily. Reigns still avoided the road but kept close enough to it that it could guide him. The route became mountainous, and at certain points Reigns climbed large boulders and pushed through thick mountain laurel. As Reigns progressed, there was a gradual increase of travelers on the road which became a steady stream. The first glimpse that Reigns had of Petronev was the city's tall, gray walls carved from the mountain.

As Reigns crept closer, still attempting to remain unseen, the mountain city stood before him. The city was quite literally the mountain, and the mountain was the city. The two were indistinguishable, as many of the structures were carved out of the rocky mountainside. The geography caused the city to slope with the mountain. As Reigns could see over the walls there were not many tall or impressive buildings, but there were innumerable small structures roughly hewn from rock. There were almost no wooden structures. The place was gray and gloomy. The few colors stemmed from fires, which in turn made the mountain city look angry and embittered. At the top of the city, there was a small, rectangular section of various-colored buildings. This must be where the affluent of the city lived.

Reigns knew the best time to get into the city and avoid suspicion was during the day. If he tried to sneak in during the night, it might lead to unwanted questions. He quickly joined one of the trickling lines walking toward a city gate. To Reigns's surprise, the line never halted but flowed continually into the city. *Shouldn't there be a checkpoint here?* As he got closer, he saw that there was, in fact, a checkpoint established, but the guards that were supposed to be manning it were occupied. The four guards for the entrance and various other travelers were gathered around two men who were fistfighting. One guard was taking bets on the spectacle. Reigns just shook his head in disbelief. He walked through the gate unnoticed and set about finding lodging for the night. *Only for one night.*

The streets were lined with small booths, each peddling likely stolen trinkets. Reigns had no interest in them. He wandered the cobblestone streets looking for a place to restock on food. He managed not to trip over any of the drunkards passed out in the streets. Reigns could have sworn some of the men weren't drunks but were dead from the previous night's bar fights. He decided to make his way to the center of the city. In this area, he would be able to find an inn for the night and to learn from the keeper where the market was. After walking awhile, he saw a vast expanse break up the monotony of buildings, like a glade far off in the forest. As Reigns approached the large, barren section of the city, he noticed it was not a clearing, but a pit. The sound of cheering emanated from the pit. Reigns was close enough to see that the hole was larger than the entire northeast barracks. It was lined with spectators and in the middle was a circular sand-covered platform where a large bull fought a severely under-armed contestant. The spectacle disgusted Reigns. He turned heel and sought an inn a few blocks away.

* * *

The sign read The Broken Bench. It was a small inn tucked between two large residential buildings. Nothing about its appearance alarmed Reigns. It was quaint and somewhat well-kept. Only a few windows were broken, which was an anomaly compared to the rowdier inns Reigns saw. *This is it. I don't want to be caught out in these streets after dark.*

Reigns walked into the Broken Bench and to his surprise, it was not like most other inns. There was no large room with a table where patrons could drink and eat. Instead, upon entering, he was in a small room with a single desk. Seated behind the desk was an elderly woman. Her hair was not white but deep gray. Her most striking feature was one large ear. Reigns did not see another.

He strode up to her confidently. "Excuse me, Miss..." Reigns extended his hand waiting for her name.

"Don't be calling me no *Miss.*" She turned and spat into a brass basin on the floor. It made a loud ding. "As for me name, I am Lethe. I presume you are wanting a room?"

"Yes...Lethe."

"I have a few left for the night. You won't cause me no trouble will ye?"

"No, I'm only in the city to resupply and spend the night."

Lethe stood. This must have been all she needed to know. She showed no signs of age but walked strong and sure from behind her desk until she was uncomfortably close to Reigns. She reached up and grabbed his collar, simultaneously yanking him down with surprising strength.

Reigns looked into her charcoal-gray eyes.

"I have one rule in my inn: if you cause trouble, I'll kill ye."

There was a brief pause. Reigns was slightly in shock to hear the threat from the small, but surprisingly strong woman.

"You'll have no problem from me, Lethe."

"Good. That will be two copper."

Reigns paid and then Lethe slapped a key into his hand and waved dismissively toward the stairs.

"Up the stairs and third room on the right. Oh, and make sure you lock your windows. We don't want trouble coming to find you."

Reigns nodded slightly and walked up the stairs.

The room was more modest than the dwellings Horace usually gave Reigns. This inn only provided the occupant with a bed. There was no other furniture. Reigns wondered if the other furnishing had been stolen or destroyed. Likewise, he did not get the sense that this was the kind of place that brought buckets of water to wash in. This did not bother him. He simply wanted to rest before continuing his journey the next day. Before retiring for the night, he made sure to close and lock the window. It made the room a great deal warmer, but he was grateful that he heeded the warning when he heard someone try to pry the window open during the night.

The night was uninterrupted, save for the erstwhile intruder. The sun was just peaking up into the window when Reigns rose. He was ecstatic to put on dry clothes. He vowed never to take dry clothes for granted again. He quickly packed and descended the stairs. There sitting behind the desk was Lethe. A man was sprawled out unconscious on the floor. There was a small puddle of blood that issued from a laceration buried in his dark hair.

Reigns motioned to the man on the floor. "Dead?"

"Not yet, but he will be soon. I'm planning to have him sent to the pit," she said.

Changing the subject, Reigns asked, "Where is the food market?"

"It is on the western wall. Can't miss it. Go to the gate and follow the main road west."

"Thank you, Lethe."

"You are welcome back to the Broken Bench anytime, as long as you follow the rule."

Reigns turned and left. This truly was a strange and lawless city. He hoped that he would never have to walk the streets of Petronev again, let alone stay overnight. Reigns counted himself lucky that he was able to find a place such as the Broken Bench. He stowed the location of the inn away in his memory, just in case he ever had to come to Petronev again.

Reigns followed the main road west from the pit. The city was beyond doubt a cesspool. There was refuse as far as the eye could see. Rats outnumbered the citizens five to one, and the smell from a long-neglected sewage system emanated from somewhere below the road. Once in the market district, he quickly resupplied on dried meats, bread, and few raw vegetables.

After only a brief, discreet visit, Reigns walked through the western gate of Petronev.

# 20

As the day came to a close, it was time for Will to meet up with Sihu. He climbed the temple stairs among a throng of people who were supposedly going to worship. An arm jutted out and pulled him to the side.

In a moment, Will was face-to-face with Sihu.

"We have to get out of here. It's not safe, Will."

Will recognized the seriousness in both her expression and the tone of her voice. He heeded her warning. The two fought the tide of the crowd to get down the steps. Luckily, Will had not made it that far up before Sihu caught him. They moved through the streets silently and swiftly. Will trusted Sihu enough to not ask questions until it was safe.

Once back at the inn and in their room, Will asked, "What is going on?"

Sihu sat down on the bed and looked at Will.

"I found out much more than I expected. First, it seems that my people are giving the empire a lot of trouble, so they decided to burn the forest. However, our trees don't burn until they're dead, so it is essentially just brush fires, which my people can handle."

Will was relieved that those he loved were alive.

Sihu continued. "Second, the temple is a temple to the Valkyn Lushian and the emperor. They worship them, and it is actually inhabited by a Valkyn. I don't know whether it is Lushian himself or another one. Third, there apparently is a man looking for you who is claiming to be your father."

Sihu pulled out a flyer and handed it to him. It was the sketch of him that he had seen once before. It had been on a wanted poster that Felix brought home from Nibridge. Will did not look much like the sketch anymore. His beard had started to grow in and his features looked more worn.

"My dad?" Will asked himself while shaking his head. Emotions boiled within him. The thought of his dad having been tortured and sent by the empire to find him made him almost lose his dinner.

"Where? Where? Did you see him?"

"Will," Sihu said, calmly.

Will began to ramble. "How did he know where to look? How did he escape? I thought he might be dead."

"Will!"

As if just realizing her presence again, he looked at her.

She spoke. "Will, I did see him, but who is to say it isn't an agent of the empire?"

*Why is she trying to take this from me?* "Well Sihu, what did he look like?" he spat at her.

Remaining calm, she said, "The man I saw handing out flyers was short and rather wide or at least he had been at some point. He was balding on top and walked with a noticeable limp."

Will's heart sank. He couldn't think of anyone he knew that walked with the limp.

"That. Is not my..." He choked on the last word. He had dared to hope for a moment that he could see his father.

"I'm sorry, Will," Sihu responded to the brief silence.

Will replied unexpectantly, "No. This imposter will be sorry. Tomorrow we are going to find him and deal with him."

"I really don't think that is wise, Will. It would probably be just playing into the empire's hand."

Will's scruffy jaw was set, teeth clenched. "I will not let *anyone* dishonor my family and father. I already had to abandon them to who-knows-what fate."

Sihu sighed, "Let's just go to bed."

That night, sleep was hard to come by. Will started on his back trying to sleep, but the inferno inside his chest was too hot. He ended up leaning against the cool wall, tossing the rocks in an attempt to calm himself. Sihu did not have much luck either. She tossed and turned. She briefly made eye contact with him, but quickly turned over to face the wall.

The sun sliced through the curtains. After the tense, quiet night, its warm rays were a relief.

Will spoke first. "You don't have to come with me. I can see you are hesitant."

Taking her time, Sihu stretched as she sat up. "Will," she said, standing up. She strode over to him and stood closer than she had ever been before.

As Will looked down into her face, she stared into his eyes. He embraced her green gaze.

"I have nowhere else to go. I made my decision to go with you. Our destiny lies together."

Will softened. "I got you something," he said, remaining cool.

"What?"

"Well, I didn't know when to give it to you, but if something happens to us, I want you to have this." He pulled out the necklace.

Sihu smiled, "I love it!" She turned her back to Will, flipped her braid with her hand, and said, "Let's see it on."

Will's hands shook slightly as he struggled with the clasp. Sihu turned around. The necklace accentuated her already-green eyes. At that moment, Will knew there was no one else with whom he would rather be stranded in a foreign city.

The two quickly packed and Will followed Sihu to the place where she had seen the old man. It made Will nervous to see so many posters of his face plastered around taverns, inns, and posts. They came to what was the main square of Fizon. It was an impossible gridlock. Using the skills learned from moving fluidly throughout the forest, they made it to the center in no time.

Off to the west side of the market, they saw a man plastering more images of Will onto building sides. He was pleading with anyone who would listen, "Please, please help me! Have you seen my son? He ran off. Please, please, please! I need to find him."

The man looked familiar, but Will couldn't quite place him from the distance. He eventually went down a side road. Will and Sihu followed him.

As the man scurried down the almost-abandoned

side street, Will broke into a full-out run. Once he closed the distance, Sihu hot on his heels, he grabbed the man's cloak and threw him up against the wall, face first. Will was surprised at his own strength.

The man screamed in pain. "Please, no! Stop! I don't have any money. I'm just looking for my son."

The statement boiled Will's blood and Will threw him to the ground.

*"Who do you think you are?"* But as Will stood over the man, he recognized a familiar face.

The face staring back at Will was a face he had loved, although it was now changed, almost feral. The man had bags under his eyes like he hadn't slept in weeks, his mouth bled, and he looked like he had aged thirty years. He did not look like the Felix that Will had seen right before he left the house.

"Will!" Felix groveled to Will's leg and hugged it.

"Felix!" Will lifted up the small man and embraced him. "Felix," he said again. "I was so worried. What happened to you? You look awful."

Felix glanced toward the ground. "It hasn't been easy. They tortured me, Will...I...I confessed everything...I...I told them where you went."

At these words, Will took a few steps back. On his knees, Felix crawled toward him.

"How could you?" Will said.

Felix's sunken, gray eyes looked at him, "I didn't have a choice."

Sihu brandished her black dagger. She spoke sternly. "Will, we need to get out of here. I don't like this."

*"No!"* Felix shouted, and he lunged toward Will, tackling him. "You have to come back with me! They

don't want to hurt you, just return you to the mountain."

"Get off me!" Will shouted.

*Thunk.* Felix's body went limp and dropped to the ground. Standing over them, Sihu brandished the hilt she had just used to incapacitate the man.

Will clambered to his feet. He stared at the now-motionless body of a man he had loved and come to see as a father figure. The man was a shadow of his former self. He had lost at least forty pounds of weight. His cloak was tattered, and he had a noticeable odor.

Sihu broke the silence. "We need to get moving before the city guard gets here."

"We can't just leave him here."

Sihu said, "Will, we can't take him with us. He betrayed you to the empire."

"I can't leave him, Sihu. Who knows what they did to him. Whatever it was, it's my fault. I interrupted his peaceful life. He is my responsibility."

Sihu helped Will hold the smelly, old man between them as they walked toward the docks.

While the sight of two young people holding up an old passed-out man between them might naturally draw attention, there were lots of drunks and stumbling through the streets near the docks. Will tracked down the captain he had hired to take them upriver.

When they got there, the old man looked skeptical. "Wut ye draggin, kids?"

"This is our uncle. He's a bit of a drunk, but I need to purchase another passage."

"Mmmm, aight, but he shan't be drinking on me boat. Pay up."

* * *

The boat swayed back and forth as Will and Sihu sat in their small quarters. Felix lay on the floor between them. Sihu twirled the black dagger in her hand while her eyes were glued to the motionless man. Will ran his hands through his black, now quite long, hair, clearly at his wit's end.

"What could they have done to him?" Will asked, rhetorically. "His only crime was helping me. It's all my fault. Look at him."

"Will, Felix made a choice, even when he knew who you were, not to turn you in. He made his decision; you did not make it for him."

"Look at him, Sihu! Look at him! This isn't Felix. This isn't how he looks or how he talks."

"I'm sorry, Will. I'm truly sorry."

The two sat in another prolonged silence. Will continued to run his hand through his hair until the old man began to stir.

Felix scanned the cabin with wide eyes, until he spotted Will. He quickly rolled onto his hands and knees and groveled toward Will. In a split second, the point of a blade was at his throat with Sihu attached to the other end. Felix glanced at her and then back to Will.

Will addressed his friend. "Felix, please sit."

The man begged, "Will, please! We don't have time. You must come with me! I've been gone too long.

"Felix! Sit down." The voice came from Will but he didn't recognize it. It was commanding and stern.

Felix rolled back and sat with his back to the wall.

"Felix, what happened to you after I fled?"

Tears streaked the broken man's face. "Will..." For

a brief second, he looked like Will's old friend. "Will, the things...the things they did to me..."

"What happened, Felix?" Will insisted.

"He tortured me. I told him everything, and then he kept torturing me until..."

"Who tortured you?"

"The emperor. He tortured me until I made him a vow. I'm sorry, Will, but you have no idea what he did to me..."

Sihu stood with a dangerous look in her eyes, "What vow did you make, old man?"

"I promised to bring Will to him..."

"And what has bound you to keep this oath?" she asked, through now-gritted teeth.

There was a pause.

"The emperor's magic, I think. I had to swear on a stone...I tried to flee to the wilderness once released, but I couldn't. Every time I try to run from my oath, I experience excruciating pain..."

Will and Sihu exchanged looks—Will's of empathy, Sihu's of realization.

She continued her questioning. "If all is as you say, then why aren't you experiencing this torture now?"

"I'm sorry, Will, I'm sorry. You see—"

Felix screamed and went into convulsions.

After it was over, he could barely speak, but he said, "I'm sorry...I tried."

Will was stunned by the power that held Felix captive. Sihu strolled over and, with a swift hit of the pommel of her dagger, Felix was unconscious once again.

"My goodness, Sihu, look at the man! Have compassion. He has suffered atrocities for the sake of our mission."

"Will, I don't like this. I don't like this at all." She did not bear her typical stoic facial expression, but one of panic. "This man and the magic over him…I know you see him as family, but something is wrong. We need to get rid of him. He is a threat to our mission."

"Sihu, I hear what you are saying. But we are on a boat headed to a destination only we know. Felix doesn't even know where we are going, so how could we be playing into the empire's hand?"

"This is stronger magic than I have ever seen, Will. It affects not only his physical body but is attuned to his very desires and intentions. The man is literally a walking, breathing, thinking pawn for the emperor. And his one goal is to bring you in. Your love for the man is blinding you, Will. You can't trust him."

"I don't trust him, and my love for him, for my people, my family, you, and your village, is what makes me who I am."

"You are right, Will. I'm sorry…I didn't mean to insult you as a person. I'm just concerned about going forward."

Will sat down beside Sihu. He placed his arm around her. She tensed slightly, but did not move away.

"It will be alright, Sihu. I won't let anything happened to you." He smiled playfully and gave her a slight squeeze.

She leaned her head until it was flush with his shoulder and rolled her eyes slightly. "My hero," she mocked, batting her eyelashes.

The two sat quietly until Will's stomach began to

gurgle.

As he tried to will his stomach from making the uncomfortable sound, Sihu said, "It must be time for dinner."

With that, she assumed a more upright position.

"I'll get dinner ready, Sihu. You relax."

For what seemed like the first time, she listened to him and sat back down. Will prepared a meager couple pieces of cheese and salted pork. He set some aside for when Felix came around. Will felt uncomfortable looking at the disheveled man.

The two finally broached the subject of what to do with Felix.

"I think we should throw him overboard and let the empire pick him up on the shore," Sihu said, only half joking.

Will more seriously said, "We need to try and free him, Sihu. I think if we can figure out how he is accomplishing his mission right now, we can start to help him."

"Yeah, but even if we do, how can we ever trust him? He serves the will of the emperor."

"He is a *slave* to the emperor."

"Alright Will, since the king has called you, I will trust your judgment. However, this one," she motioned to the snoring man, "is on a very short rope."

# 21

Three days passed since Reigns left Petronev. He kept thinking about how he never wished to enter its premises again, but a sneaking suspicion told him that he would one day go back. Reigns spent much of his time going over all of the details and roads he had encountered in the city. His military training had taught him to keep a good sense of recall. He could never know which information was vital, and it would be a mighty shame if he had once known something but could not remember it.

Reigns's journey was easier and much quicker-paced once leaving Petronev. He decided to travel by road because most of the soldiers who would recognize him served primarily east of Petronev, and even if they saw him, his unkempt appearance and stubbly beard would mask his identity. The empire was also going to war against the rebels of the Dark Forest and it would be a poor use of resources to spend too much time looking for an AWOL soldier. Last, and most importantly, was the need to hurry. Reigns did not have a specific date to meet this mysterious boy, but he could not risk missing him.

In his dreams, Reigns tried on numerous occasions to discuss with the king in further detail his role or mission, but it never moved past his agreement to meet the boy. Reigns could not afford to miss the person he had sacrificed his career, farm, and friendships for.

The road that Reigns now traveled was known as Bandit's Road. It bordered the northern edge of the Miklak Desert. The road wound and weaved through giant boulders and had a number of bridges over deep crevices that appeared to have no bottoms. It was prime territory for highway robbers to hide and ambush unsuspecting travelers. Already Reigns had run into numerous groups traveling east who had been ambushed. Those who traveled the road often carried an extra portion of coin to pay off the robbers, but those who did not were lucky if they were allowed to keep the clothes on their backs. The army's patrols were essentially useless. Lookouts sent warnings to those waiting in ambush and the bandits would vanish. Reigns knew this because of the headaches they had caused his commanding officers stationed in the northern Miklak barracks.

Reigns had attached himself to a group of five other travelers. They were merchants who sought the cheap prices of stolen goods in Petronev and planned to turn them into large profits by selling to those in Tizon, the capital. Reigns found it ironic that they were likely selling the various trinkets to the very people that they had been stolen from. He did not speak to others except when necessary. In attempting to keep a low profile, he kept his conversations to the most trivial subjects, such as the weather, or gossip about the court.

One night, as the group sat around the fire, Reigns began to drift off until he heard something that piqued his interest.

"They say the Dwellers are putting up quite a fight, killed two Valkyns last I heard."

*Dwellers* was a name used by the folk in the empire to speak about the inhabitants of the Dark Forest.

"I heard it was four," another interjected.

"Keep your voices down," the group leader hissed. "If anyone hears you speaking about those things in such an excited tone, we could be tried as sympathizers or traitors."

"Why are we even at war with the Dwellers? I thought we had a treaty or something like that. At least as long as I have been alive, I haven't heard of them causing any trouble."

They were all speaking in a very hushed tone.

"They say that they have a weapon that could destroy the emperor."

There was a brief pause.

"Shut your mouth, Tigen. No one can kill the emperor; he is invincible. Not even the old king could defeat him."

"Then why start a war for no reason?" Tigen responded.

"The emperor probably wants to keep the army on its toes, you know. That's just how ruling types are, always needing a war to fight."

The group leader spoke again. "What kind of weapon? Some sort of sorcery?"

Tigen responded in a voice barely above a whisper, "I don't know, but there are talks of the emperor going off his hinges as of late. He almost torched that small mountain town, Nibridge, I think it is called."

Reigns spoke now, "I don't mean to intrude on your very interesting conversation, but isn't this all just rumors and conjecture?"

Tigen scoffed, "I'm no gossip. I heard from me brother-in-law who serves as the tailor for the Count of Petronev."

The conversation was cut short due to another group of travelers coming into the cove to set up camp. Reigns thought it was quite encouraging for, whatever movement he was a part of, that people in the very northernmost regions of the empire were already discussing the "weapon" or, as he knew him, Will.

The following days went by without incident, without bandits or ambushes, though Reigns knew that they passed through the ambushes of two gangs.

When he asked Tigen why he thought they hadn't seen any bandits, Tigen pointed to the group leader and said, "See that gold-and-red band around his arm?"

"Yes."

"He bought safe passage for this road while we were in Petronev. He will return the armband once we get to Tizon."

Reigns was quite impressed by the organization of the criminal network in this area. No wonder the army had such difficulty dealing with the bandits. Whoever was running the criminal network was smart and must be well-positioned.

The road that the group traveled passed through a small development called the Northwest Outpost, where the army barracks for this region was located. It was generally perceived to be a safe place to rest for weary travelers. Reigns's supplies were still in good count, thanks to the generosity of his traveling companions at mealtimes. Reigns saw the outpost as an unnecessary risk. Even though he braved the roads as an army deserter, going right into the heart of one of the empire barracks was not wise. He bid farewell to his companions. Tigen pulled him aside and gave him directions to his home in Tizon.

"I'm not sure what your business is in Tizon, but if you need a place to stay, come to my home. I may not know much about you, but you are at least an honorable man, as far as I have been able to tell."

Reigns was grateful for the offer but insisted he would be fine. However, he locked the location in his memory in case he had need in the future.

As Reigns circumvented the outpost by taking farm paths and game trails, he constantly thought about the information he had received. The emperor was distraught over Will. Reigns knew the kid was powerful based on what he did to the Valkyn at Felix's house, but for the emperor to start a war over capturing him? This gave all the credibility that he needed to the king who visited him in his dreams. Reigns knew he was doing the right thing. He might yet be able to make this world he lived in a better place for Sophie. He just hoped that he could survive the oncoming war and see that world himself.

Back on a main road, he traveled the last two days south to Tizon on his own and undetected. At least, so he thought.

* * *

Tizon was the largest city in the empire. Reigns had spent considerable time stationed there as a soldier in his younger days. It was the only city to have four barracks that surrounded it, one on each side. It had not changed much in the decade since he had last visited. The number of people always reminded him of ants after he kicked over an ant pile. He was astounded how so many people could fit into such a confined space.

Reigns entered the city at its northern gate. His plan was to regularly walk the main roads and busiest areas of the city and to hopefully run into Will. Reigns was able to recall the poorly sketched image he carried while searching for Will in Nibridge. He hoped the boy was smart enough to have changed his appearance before walking into the emperor's personal domain. For that matter, Reigns hoped he himself could go undetected. He had gone the extra length of purchasing a black wig with long, braided hair from a vendor just outside the city walls. Reigns entered the city under an alias and said he was looking for work.

Once into Tizon, he pretended that the grandness of the city seemed to overwhelm him. Reigns had an idea of which part of the city to stay, but it took him twice as long as he thought it should have to reach it. The area was in one of the poorest parts, called the Slum of Santra. No person of any standing or wealth would be caught dead in that area. If they were seen entering the that area of the city, a city guard was to report it and their wealth was to be stripped from them. As a result, only the poorest and most desolate individuals lived there. It fit Reigns's alias and further decreased the chance that anyone would recognize him there. If one of the empire's soldiers entered, not on orders, they were immediately discharged and branded with a hot iron to show all who saw what dishonoring the empire resulted in.

Once in the Slum of Santra, Reigns was reminded immediately of Petronev. Bodies littered the street alongside human refuse. Reigns found a small inn and rented a room. This room's only furnishing was a small mat made of cloth on the floor. Reigns knew the reason was to limit the rampant spread of fleas and rats. Even so, he chose to sleep on a different portion of the floor, laying out his cloak for a bed. He did not want to risk whatever else might inhabit the mat. He nodded off to sleep, secure in the knowledge that he had come to Tizon unnoticed by any who wished to do him harm.

As he slept, the king did not visit him in his dreams. Once this realization hit him, even in his dream, his blood pressure rose and the drumming of it in his ears woke him. When he opened his eyes, he saw a black figure standing in his room in front of the closed door. Reigns tried to lunge for his sword, but his body was unresponsive. He tried again. And again. The black figure stepped closer, though the steps on the clay floor made no sound.

"Sorcerer!" Reigns cursed through his teeth.

The dark figure cocked its head and spoke. "Is that how you speak to your emperor, Reigns, previously of the northeast barracks and now deserter and traitor of the empire?"

The voice sent a chill through Reigns's body. It was as if the emperor's voice took the heat from the room.

"Do you really think it is so easy to betray me, to betray your empire? You made an oath to serve the leader of this land, an oath of blood. You cannot evade me. You, Reigns, belong to me."

Reigns started to speak but his words caught in his throat.

The emperor held a hand up. "I know that you are seeking the boy, Will. You think that he is powerful and can overthrow me, but know this: I will find him and I will kill him. If you cooperate, the same fate will not befall your precious wife, Elana, and your daughter, Sophie. By your actions, you have already forfeited your own life, but you could still save them. Here is what you must do in order to save them. First, you will find Will and convince him of your loyalty by whatever means necessary. Second, you will find out who his accomplices are, and any strategic information concerning Will's plans, and for infiltrating the Dark Forest. Once you have enough information, you will come to my castle and report back to me. If the information you provide is significant, I will spare your family. If you prove you can be a continued asset, I may let you live until you become a burden. Know this, if you attempt to deceive me, I will know. If I find that you betray me again, you will suffer more than any other mortal has suffered in the history of this empire."

The emperor walked closer and grabbed Reigns's hand. The touch shot a painful fire through his body, but he was unable to scream. The emperor then slid an onyx ring over his right ring finger. Once on, it felt as though the ring bit into his flesh.

"This will let me terminate you at any point. You cannot run from me, Reigns."

At those final words, Reigns blacked out.

When he woke, the sun was already shining brightly through his window. Reigns thought the previous night's encounter was simply a nightmare, but when he looked at his hand, he saw a cold, onyx ring staring back at him.

# 22

The boat listed softly as it became flush with the dock in Tizon's harbor. The gangplank bridged the short chasm and the travelers disembarked. Will had to take a few steps before his feet were steady. He took the scene in and made his way onto the main thoroughfare of the harbor.

There were more ships than he could count, of every size and shape. The harbor itself was hollowed out from a gray hillside with the city above them. All the docks attached to one main road, with carts and people bustling and pushing, trying to get through. The people mostly wore tattered garments, either worn from old age or too much sun exposure on the ships. The harbor had much the same smell as Fizon. The rank odor of fish was nauseating, but it did not seem to bother anyone else there.

The trio walked along the dock road toward a large incline that was the road to the city currently towering over them. As they came to the crest of the incline, they caught their first glimpse of Tizon through one of the gates. Will had been impressed by the magnitude of Fizon, but this city existed on an entirely different plane. If they were twins, this one got all the looks.

The city was dense and cramped, with some buildings climbing higher than some of the surrounding hills. The buildings were tall and very wide, many having windows spaced evenly apart. They were built in a way that reminded Will of a honeycomb. This type of construction poked up everywhere from behind the city's gray walls. The walls alone must have been ten times Will's height. One building caught Will's eyes. Almost buried by the surrounding structure, but in what Will had to assume was the center of the city, was a large, metallic-gold palace.

Felix said, "That's the palace of the Eternal King, where the emperor resides."

Will didn't respond but ogled at its beauty.

Sihu snapped Will out of his trance. "I think we should make camp outside of the city. We don't know this place, and after all," she pointed to a towering isolated mountain in the distance, "that is where we are going."

Will squinted to get a better view. "That is where the king is being held?"

Felix jumped in, "Yes, but if you want to get there you will have to kill me. I fear that I will be forced to stop you, and— *Ahhhhhh!*".

Felix dropped to the ground, breathing heavily. The crowd slowed around them and looked on, concerned.

Sihu acted quickly. "Come on, Uncle! This is no time for your antics."

She gracefully swooped down, pulled his arm over her shoulder, and led him forward. This seemed to satisfy the crowds curiosity. As they got closer to the main gate of the city, Sihu led them from the crowded street down a road leading from the city toward the forest that bordered the River Grenvale.

Sihu let Felix down gently, which Will appreciated, then abruptly pulled Will in close. "Will, we are being followed."

"What? I didn't see anyone. Who is it?"

"I don't know, but ever since Felix had his 'moment,' someone has been following us. Will, we should just leave him."

"I hear you, Sihu. Just give me tonight to think it over."

"I will keep watch. You try and get some rest."

Will got the sense that she was not confident in Will's ability to keep watch with an enemy in their midst and another enemy following them, especially with the emperor only a short run away. Will was grateful that he had her. He knew her strengths and truly appreciated what she contributed to their quest.

There would be no fire that night. Felix lay on the ground parallel to a fallen tree, and Will slumped against a standing oak nearby. As Will fell asleep, his eyes regularly drifted toward Sihu standing watch.

*Crack!* A stick snapped, and Will's eyes flashed open, his heart drumming loudly in his ears. He saw a man standing over Felix with a knife out. Will half believed it was a dream and blinked his eyes to alleviate the sleepiness. When they opened again, the man's hands were raised. Sihu stood behind him, her left hand on his forehead pulling his head back, while her right hand pinned her blade to his neck. If Will didn't know better, he might have thought they were statues.

Will got to his feet and grabbed one of the magical rocks he always carried on him.

Felix rolled onto his back and looked the hooded man in the face, "It's *you*! No, no, NO!" The old man scrambled away trying to get to his feet. He stood behind Will. Felix spat toward the man, "Come to finish the job? The emperor said I was safe!"

Thoroughly confused, Will interrupted, "What is going on here? How do you know each other?"

"That demon," said Felix, pointing a shaky finger at the intruder, "was the one who delivered me to the emperor! He is the reason I am the way I am."

"And what way are you?" the stranger queried.

"Who are you, and why are you following us?" Will said.

"He is part of the army! They destroyed everything—my house, my farm, my books!"

"Why don't you let me answer the boy?" the strange man said. "My name is Reigns. Up until quite recently, I was a lieutenant in the imperial army."

"How recently?" Sihu asked.

Will felt a chill in her words.

"I left the army three weeks ago. I am now a wanted man being tracked by the empire. Sound familiar?"

Felix had enough. "Lies, lies, lies! You serve the emperor! You destroy people's lives and deliver them to be tortured. I wasn't a bad man!" Felix's rage was reaching new levels.

Reigns turned his head toward Felix, who was

cowering behind Will. The slight movement caused Sihu's dagger to cut slightly into his neck, but he did not flinch. The man had a strong jaw and was bearded with black hair. His hair was longer than was common and was parted to one side.

"And you, Felix, what is your purpose here? Are you not attempting to lead these two to be captured and tortured, sharing in your fate? Can you really take the moral high ground? I was simply doing my job, but you, you betrayed them."

Felix slumped, averting his eyes.

"Will, let's just kill them both and be on our way," Sihu said, as if it was the obvious decision. There was no hint of sarcasm in her suggestion.

"Why should we keep you alive?" Will asked Reigns

"Because the king sent me. Also, I can help you with him," he said, pointing at Felix.

"The king sent you? How do we know?"

"You could ask him yourself when we get there. All I can tell you is that he came to me in dreams and has refused to leave. As for Felix, he is under the influence of a Marclin Stone."

"Marclin Stones do not exist. What do you take us for, fools?" Sihu said.

"Well, there is a simple way to prove it," Reigns said. "Have that old man take his tunic off."

At that moment, Felix tried to sprint away, but Will tackled him. "Get off of me! Get off of me!" He shouted loudly, until a boot descended on his head, leaving him unconscious.

The boot belonged to Reigns.

"Was that really necessary? I'm not sure how many more blows to the head he can endure," Will asked, and caught a slight smirk coming from Sihu.

"If he keeps on shouting, he will alert our presence to other travelers, or worse, to the patrols," Reigns said.

Will rolled his eyes. "Alright, Reigns, let's see this stone."

Reigns used a small dagger drawn from somewhere on his person to cut a slit in the middle of Felix's tunic. There in the center of his back was a circular stone of a purple hue. It had black edges. Emitting from the stone was charring that seemed to be crawling up Felix's back, as if it were slowly overtaking him.

"This is very dark magic," Sihu warned, almost whispering it to Will. She now stood close to him. Her bow drawn on Reigns.

"What is that thing doing?" Will asked, motioning to the rock.

"It is controlling him. Forcing him to do the emperor's bidding. Though, it only works if the initiate is willing to originally submit to its power. After that, the stone takes over. Even if he regretted his decision he could not lapse on his commitment." Reigns explained.

"How do we remove it?"

"I do not know, outside of the commitment being fulfilled. If you look at the charring, you can see that he has been trying to fight it. Every time he goes against it, it slowly takes over him. And if he resists too much, it will kill him."

"Well, we have to try to get it off of him," Will said.

Sihu spoke next. "Will, this does not seem wise."

"It might not be, but it is the right thing to do."

Will reached toward the rock and Reigns grabbed his hand. "Kid, maybe you should listen to the girl. I have given up everything to find you, and I won't let you die within the first few minutes. If you touch that rock, it just as likely will kill both you and the old man."

"I'm no kid, and I will do what I believe to be right."

Reigns buried his head in his hands.

Will placed his hand on the Marclin Stone. Suddenly, a dark purple light poured from the rock and illuminated Will's face. The prickling started at Will's fingertips as he grasped the rock. A burning crept up his veins until his whole body felt as though it was on fire. Will refused to release his grip and doubled down. Felix was more than just a friend to him. If Will couldn't help him, how was he supposed to help his family or Sihu's people? He had to do it, not just for Felix, but for them as well. Something heavy seemed to have hit his back in the struggle. He turned to see if Reigns had attacked. Instead of an assailant, he saw a blue, translucent wing on each side of him. He gave one final heave. The stone broke free from Felix's back.

Standing back, Reigns took in the sight. "Those tattoos...wings. A blue Valkyn?" he muttered in astonishment.

Will looked at the stone in his hand and clenched his fist around it, dissolving the rock into dust that poured through his fingers. He looked at each of his wings curiously, he twitched what he thought was a back muscle and saw the wing moved. He twitched another and the other wing moved. Will tried both at once and saw the leaves on the ground move in the wind he created. Remembering his readings in the Valkyn book originally given by Felix, he placed both hands flat together and moved them from his face to his chest. In an instant, the wings were gone. Attempting the other motion represented in the book, Will took his hands at his chest and placed them together and rotated the right with the thumb interlocking until both palms faced him. The wings were back.

Sihu and Reigns stood with eyes wide and mouths open.

"Will!" Sihu shouted, "That is amazing, but the other Valkyns will be able to spot you easily."

"Right!" Will said, and he did the motion and again his wings disappeared. He looked to his old friend. Where the rock had been, there was a cauterized divot. The old man began to stir, and Will and Reigns helped him into a sitting position. He opened his eyes and they were gray but soft. They no longer held a tortured malice.

"Will," he said so softly it was almost inaudible.

"Don't say anything, Felix. You are free from your oath. I destroyed the stone."

"But how?" His voice again was not much more than a whisper.

Will gave him a boyish smile, "I'm a Valkyn."

Felix closed his eyes peacefully, as if Will's words confirmed a long-held suspicion.

The dawn began to break, and the companions had a small, dry breakfast.

Reigns approached Felix. "Felix, I truly am sorry for what happened to you. I really was just following orders as I always have. In truth, some of the reason I decided to heed the king's call was because of the injustice done to you."

Felix looked at him. "I understand why you did what you did to me, and I do not hold that against you, but I'm not quite ready to forgive you. In time, though, I hope to."

"It also seems that we have a mutual friend, Horace the innkeeper of the Windy Sun. Or at least he was the innkeeper before the empire took him."

A flash of fear ran across Felix's face. "Don't worry, I was able to free him from imprisonment right before I came in search of Will. He is safe, as far as I know, in hiding."

"Why did they take him?"

"He apparently had been dealing in books and other banned material."

"Ah, that is sad to hear. Information is one of the most powerful weapons we have against the empire."

Reigns pondered the statement a moment and rubbed his bearded chin, "Yes. Yes, it is."

As the group finished their breakfast, a startling howl broke through the early morning air.

"Wolves!" Reigns said under his breath. Raising his voice, he spoke, "There is no escape except to kill the empire's wolves. They will not relent until they have us cornered."

Another howl issued from the woods and then a whole chorus of howls joined in. They must have found the scent they sought. This was not the meager pack that Will had originally encountered.

Sihu took charge. "Will, you and Reigns get Felix out of here! I'll take care of as many wolves as I can."

"No, Will. You take Felix yourself. I will stay and help Sihu. There is a little creek on the east side of the forest. Follow it upstream until you come to a small waterfall. There is a cavern behind the falls which you should be able to hide in. The water should take care of any scent you leave behind."

Will was trying to come up with a logical reason for him to stay over the veteran soldier and the very adept Sihu, when simultaneously Reigns and Sihu shouted, "Go!"

With that, Will threw Felix's arm around his shoulder and half walked, half ran, with the recovering man. Will took one final glance back toward Sihu and Reigns, as they finished a brief conversation they were having and took off into the woods, Sihu to the northeast and Reigns to the southwest. Will focused on getting to the cave as quickly as possible. He briefly heard men shouting, but the howling of the wolves drowned them out. *I really hate those things*, he thought to himself.

After an hour or so, Felix and Will came to the creek. They navigated it until they came to a cove with a waterfall. Will, however, did not see the cave Reigns had spoken of. As they edged closer to the waterfall there was a small opening behind the falling water. Will got close and stuck his head in. Once through the opening, a meager cavern appeared. Will climbed the whole way in and pulled Felix through as he was a bit too large to fit easily through the hole. As they sat, backs against the cool wall, breathing in the moist, heavy air, Will thought of Sihu.

# 23

Minutes were hours and hours were days. Internally, Will groaned and fought his strongest desire to go in search of his friends. The only break from the torturous silence was when one of the wolves let out a howl right outside the cave, but it did not get close enough to notice the cavern's existence. Felix had not spoken the entire time. He simply rested with his eyes closed, leaning the back of his head against the wall of the cavern. Will paced the cramped expanse, seemingly trying to wear a rut into the hard stone.

Well after dark, an arm came through the entrance to the cave. Will jumped. Another arm, and then the head of Reigns appeared. He hoisted himself through the narrow opening. His hair, which had been so kempt that morning, was disheveled. He now bled from his right forearm, and his face bore the scratches of thickets.

Immediately, a look of panic crossed his face and he asked, "Where is the girl? She should have been here hours ago."

Will's heart sank. "We haven't seen her. What

happened out there?"

Reigns sat down with a thud, his small pack and weapons making a clanging sound.

"This is isn't good."

"What's not good?"

"If she is not here, then she has either been killed or worse, taken captive. I do not believe that the orders were to kill, especially since the empire is at war with her people. The empire will probably skip bribing her for information and start with torture."

Will's eyes watered, not out of sadness but out of anger at himself for the situation.

Felix spoke, "You have to save her. You have no idea what they are capable of. Not even you, soldier." Felix's eyes seemed to sink into his skull as he spoke, and shadows moved across his eyes, "There were times..." he gulped, "...that the emperor forced the guards to leave, so that he could..."

"It's okay, Felix. We understand. That won't happen to her. We are going after her!"

Reigns eyes met Will's. "Is she worth it? Everything that has happened, everything I gave up, everything she is suffering, everything that Felix suffered for, it will all be for naught if you get captured."

"I would never leave her in the hands of the empire. She knows that, and I would die trying to save her."

"Alright. Felix, you will be of no help to us in your present state. I think it would be best if you went and stayed with our old friend, Horace."

Felix hesitated, then gave in, "I'm... still pretty shook up. You're probably right."

After the consensus, the three began developing a

plan based on the likely locations that the soldiers would have taken Sihu.

Felix was not much help as he had never been to the capital before, but Reigns offered invaluable insight, "The army has three barracks around Tizon, and as far I know, the regular city guard has no access to the wolves. Because of that, I assume we will find her awaiting interrogation at one the barracks...at least until the emperor returns."

"Wouldn't the army just hand her over to the city guard? Also, how do you know the emperor isn't there?" Will asked.

"The army and city guards have no love for each other, and with such a valued prisoner, the army would never let her out of their control. And when the emperor is in the city, the guards are doubled at the gate. When I came through, it appeared as though they had their usual detachment."

Reigns, in his duties, had visited the barracks on numerous occasions. Using his memories of the place, the three finalized their plan.

Reigns gave instructions to Felix on how to find his family and Horace. Felix's torn and tattered clothes made him look all the more the role of the weary traveler. Once Felix was off, Reigns and Will left the cave, leaving anything that wasn't necessary for the night. Implementing their plan would require stealth and, hopefully, little bloodshed. Though Reigns had forsaken the army he once admired, many of the men would do the same once they realized the injustice within its ranks. It would not do to harm anyone who might become an ally in the future.

* * *

Will and Reigns approached the second barracks, as the first had yielded no results. Each of the barracks was stationed about a half hour walk from the city. There was one each to the north, east, and south. The western side of the city was bordered by the vast Grenvale River, and thus the navy was responsible for its security. They had initially started at the southern barracks. After a brief observation, it became evident that the soldiers were much too lax to be in charge of a highly wanted captive. When they came to the eastern barracks, there was a stark contrast. The earthen and stone walls were patrolled vigilantly. In addition to a soldier standing every couple of yards, there were continuous patrols passing every three minutes or so.

This particular barracks was stationed in the center of a large clearing. The forest and greenery were easily visible to the west, and the desert was clear and vast to the east. Additionally, King's Mountain dominated the horizon. The sun was just beginning to peek from the other side of the mountain which made it seem even more dominating.

Reigns turned to Will. "When the tip of the mountain's shadow touches the western wall, that will be our signal."

The man then snuck off in the dewy grass moving toward the western side of the barracks. He moved stealthily through the woods, though not quite as skillfully as Sihu's people. Will was about to take the most dangerous risk of his life. He was about to be the distraction to draw the attention of the entire barracks.

Will crept as close to the southern gate as he could

without being detected. The magical dust was beginning to disappear with the encroaching daylight. He took the time to form ten large rocks and five smaller ones, which is all that would fit in his pocket. As the tip of the mountain's shadow was almost on the wall, he unwrapped the sling that he and Reigns had quickly made. It was a small piece of leather with two strips of cloth attached to it. Ordinarily, Will's heart would have been beating out of his chest, but he was calm and cool. He kept one thing in his mind, and if his mind started to wander, he focused again. *Sihu.*

The shadow touched the western wall. Will stood behind the tree, placed the now-invisible explosive in the sling, and spun it. After attaining momentum, he released. His ears seemed to tighten as he braced for the sound. *Boom!* The entire gate blew to pieces. Screams and shouts came from the barracks. *Boom!* Another projectile struck the southern wall, critically damaging it. Will heard the clink and clank of soldiers' armor as they came from where their gate had once stood. Will launched another projectile. *Boom!* The wall fell in on itself after two hits.

"There he is!" A soldier shouted.

*Thunk! Thunk, thunk, thunk!* Arrows hit the tree Will was standing behind. He risked throwing one more of the large rocks, but as soon as he exposed his position, arrows came at him and he faltered. The rock fell a few yards short of its target. *Boom!* A large crater resulted. Will picked up the last of the large, invisible rocks and retreated farther south into the wood.

After he was out of the range of the soldiers'

arrows, Will dared to look back. The soldiers were standing in formation outside the barracks, but they were not pursuing him. *What are they waiting for?* Will heard a blood-curdling howl, followed by a chorus of other howls. The barracks had released the creatures from the eastern gate, and they were in a full-out sprint coming toward him. Will counted five wolves, but the thing that concerned him more was the Valkyn flying close behind them. The wolves were the immediate threat and would be on him in moments. Will placed the last large stone into the sling, leading the beasts as best he could, and launched the stone. *Boom!* Another crater formed to the sounds of yelps and howls from the injured wolves. There was still one sprinting toward him.

Will pulled his sword from its scabbard, placing it in his left hand. He withdrew a handful of the small stones from his pocket. The wolf launched from a full sprint into the air. As the beast jumped, Will slid under its enormous body. The wolf landed and pivoted. Will threw the fistful of small stones. They exploded around the wolf, though they were not large enough to kill the creature. Once thrown, Will switched his sword to his dominant hand and charged the thoroughly disoriented beast. With a single motion, Will ended it's life.

As the wolf contacted the ground with a heavy thud, Will heard a battle cry from above him. Instinctually, he elevated his sword and blocked the strike from the Valkyn. Again and again they parried, the Valkyn taking large swings as if he would break Will's sword in two. Will had never fought with someone above him. After a few exchanges, the Valkyn backed up a few feet and landed, staring at Will.

The Valkyn was hideous. His face was tattooed, but his tattoos were random and disorganized as if a wild beast had attacked a man's face, leaving scars. The Valkyn wore black, metallic armor. In his right hand, he wielded a hand-and-a-half sword which glowed a faint, red color. This red was matched by his wings. They were solid wings, not translucent, like Will's.

The Valkyn spoke, "Spawn of the cursed, yield to me and you might yet live. The emperor desires your presence." The beast's voice made it sound like he had a chest full of gravel.

The fire of righteous indignation that burned inside Will had been escalating since he first set eyes on the Valkyn. Now, having heard it speak in a tone that would have made a child cry, a cool fire burned through his veins to every extremity.

"Spawn of the *cursed?"* Will spat back at the creature. "Have you looked in a mirror recently? You betrayed our kind, and for what? Your own selfish desire."

"Silence, cursed one!" the Valkyn hissed, his face now contorting. "You have no right to claim the Valkyn name, for your people have been cursed to forever endure a flightless, meaningless existence. And I, I am a god amongst men. I am worshiped."

Will had had enough of the creature's words and arrogance. He did the quick hand-motion and his wings burst from his back. He felt as though he'd released the creature within him, and it felt good to be free. The other Valkyn took a few steps back at Will's transformation. Will's sword glowed a faint blue, contrasting with the enemy's red weapon.

Words rolled from Will's tongue without him knowing where they came from, nor being able to stop them. "You are no longer a Valkyn. Your treason and evil have transformed you. While once you were beautiful and served with honor, you have become corrupted and deformed. I name you and your kind *Illkyn,* and you will fall!" Will knew the words to be right and true. Though they came from his mouth, he did not expect to speak with such authority.

The Illkyn let out a battle cry and lurched into the air. A rush of wind broke over Will's face as the Illkyn took off. He came down hard with his blade toward Will.

Will blocked and dove forward into a role. Though his wings should have hindered this, they did not. It was as if they had not been there. Standing, Will launched himself into the air. He had only meant to jump but he continued upward as if gliding. Will dove toward the Illkyn, swiping with his blade as he flew past. Quickly realizing he was on a trajectory to smash into the ground, Will leaned back and flapped steadily. He remained suspended at a steady height in the air, and looked toward the Illkyn.

The hideous beast was not flying steadily. In fact, he was retreating toward the barracks. He flapped a few times, then quickly descended as he half-ran, half-flew back to the barracks, like a bird with a broken wing. A piece of red wing laid on the ground. Though Will could barely see the soldiers' faces, they stood with their mouths agape.

"Archers, archers, shoot! Shoot him!" the Illkyn screamed.

Will took this time to make a flying retreat south a few leagues. Once a safe distance away, he did a hand motion and his wings went away. He hiked for an hour back to the hidden cave. Squeezing through the tiny hole, he spied the loveliest sight he had ever set eyes on: Sihu.

Sihu had taken a beating at the hands of the army. She bore a large gash on the right side of her forehead, presumably from where she was struck by one of her captors. Her left eye was turning a deep purple, similar to the color of the magic dust. Despite her injuries, she wore a split-lipped smile when she looked at him.

"Will!" she said in a raspy voice.

"Sihu! Are you okay? Did they hurt you badly?"

Reigns responded for her. "She will be alright. She has a few broken ribs and a bite from one of the wolves on her left calf, but nothing is of a serious nature."

Her raspy voice interjected again. "You should not have come for me. It was not wise."

Will closed the expanse between them and took Sihu's chin in his hand. As he knelt, he stared her in the eyes. "Sihu, did you really believe that we were not going to come for you?"

A small tear trickled from her eye.

She started to speak but seemed to choke on the words. Then with a small smile, she said, "I never doubted you would come for me."

The conversation appeared to be taxing on Sihu. Will retrieved some water for her, and then she went to sleep. Reigns was standing at the entrance to the cave. Will walked over to him and leaned against the wall.

Reigns looked at Will, seeming to size him up as

warriors often do with each other. "You made quite the distraction," Reigns said.

"I followed our plan, but I was not expecting an Illkyn or the wolves."

"An Illkyn?" Reigns asked, puzzled.

"It is the name for corrupted Valkyns. They no longer receive the honorable name. What happened inside the barracks?"

"I was in position when you started the barrage. As soon as you blew through the wall and all the soldiers turned their attention to the south, I was able to scale the northern wall and drop in. Sihu was in the prisoners' quarters. Since there is only one entrance, I had to wait for the time right. Luckily, another soldier came and said that two Valkyns were fighting. It must have been one of the guardsman's buddies because they took off together to see the show. I snuck in and was able to untie Sihu. We snuck out through the northern gate and came back here. Despite her injuries, she was still silent and quick through the woods. It wasn't until we got back here that we were able to assess her injuries. How did you defeat the Illkyn?"

Will stated matter-of-factly, "He underestimated me."

"That's all?" Reigns scoffed.

"I doubt that the next time I face one of the Illkyn it will be so careless. I need to train for aerial combat if I am going to survive the coming war."

The following morning, Reigns left to scout their route while Will helped Sihu get ready for travel. He wrapped a cloth tightly around her ribs and gave her some of the dried meat that they had bought in Fizon. Fizon seemed like it had happened years ago, rather than a few days ago. Sleep had done wonders for Sihu's recovery. After the meager breakfast, she instructed Will on how to make the healing paste he had needed just a few weeks earlier.

He followed her instructions, pouring strange-smelling dried foliage into a cup and mixing it with water to form a paste. Using his fingers, Will scooped some of the paste out. It felt cold but soothing to his touch. He guided the deep, green, viscous liquid over the cut on her forehead, and then on her calf. She neither winced nor showed any sign of pain, but instead, she stared at Will. He was holding every ounce of her attention.

Will tried not to meet Sihu's gaze. This was the closest he had ever been to her, or to any girl, and did not want to offend her. It was futile. As he finished the application, he dared to take a glance. Instantly, he was captivated. He had always known her eyes were charming and green, but now he saw them up close. They were emeralds. Beautiful, surpassing anything he had yet seen in this life. They were deep and knowing, as if he could dive into them. Will felt something warm touch his hand. It was Sihu's hand. He took it between his and pulled it into his chest.

Sihu leaned forward until her forehead rested against his lips. Time stood still. Nothing else mattered in that moment. It was as if he forgot everything that had happened, and all that would happen. All that mattered was this moment, this woman, here and now.

"Ugh-hum." The noise echoed around the cave and Will pulled her in close to protect her from any potential threat.

"It's just me, Will," Reigns said, with a playful grin on his face.

"What—" Will's voice cracked awkwardly and he gathered himself. "What does the path look like?" Will wished he could smack the wry grin off Reigns's face.

"Primarily archers patrolling all of the roads and any well-traveled path. We would do best to stay off the trail and take our time to sneak through the woods."

"That sounds like most of the traveling we do anyway," Will commented offhandedly.

"I'm most comfortable traveling that way," Sihu said, while squeezing Will's hand slightly.

Will and Reigns split Sihu's pack between them so that she would be able to have her full range of motion. They began to move soundlessly through the woods. If a patrol did not see them, they had no hope of finding them. More than once, they passed by animals without causing them to stir. Will thought Fox would be proud of how silent their group moved through the woods.

They made it to the desert's edge with plenty of time to spare before dark and decided it would be best to camp in the tree canopy, in case a patrol came through. Will and Reigns placed a number of limbs across some branches to form a narrow, hardly noticeable, platforms as Sihu kept watch. That night they did not talk, nor did Will sleep. While Sihu looked content in the elevated bed, Reigns tied himself down with a small string. Will feared rolling off and wished he had taken Reigns up on his offer for some of the cord. He settled for a half-awake, half-asleep state of mind. The trio only rested for a few hours before waking so that they could travel through the desert by night, thus avoiding prying eyes that would have easily seen them moving during the day. In an effort to avoid identification by the Illkyn, both Will and Sihu wrapped fabric, with cut eye holes, around their head.

# 24

The desert was a floor of beige sand broken up by a variety of plants that neither Will nor Sihu had ever laid eyes on. The extra energy it took to take each step as the sand gave way felt funny at first, but quickly grew wearisome. A cool night breeze crossed the three as they trekked silently through the unfamiliar terrain. The sun broke the horizon and the mountain prison now looked twice as big as it had from the barracks.

The group decided that it would be best to rest during the day and make the final push toward the mountain at night. With the sun still low, they found a small crevice and threw some dried twigs across it, and their traveling cloaks on top. As they sat in the small cavern, their shoulders touched.

Although out of the sun, the heat was almost unbearable. As sweat poured off of them, they passed a water skin around. None of them were in a mood to expend the energy to talk. Their minds were on their imminent meeting with the king who had called Will and Reigns. Sihu was especially nervous about the meeting. What would the king say to her?

The king had not contacted her specifically, but she decided on her own to go.

The evening shadows slowly crept over the hot desert. The travelers put their cloaks on and traveled toward King's Mountain. All was going smoothly, when high above them a meteor flashed, but did not disappear. Its red glow lingered in an unnaturally steady light.

"You two get down!" Reigns hissed.

The two dropped, realizing if they looked up, the Illkyn would see their eyes.

Reigns quickly threw his dirty, dark cloak over Will's and Sihu's faces to ensure they were not spotted. Reigns watched the red dot fade as it flew toward King's Mountain.

Once Reigns was sure the Illkyn would not spot them, they continued their travels. They crept silently for a few more hours before they could see the lamp fires of the guard towers on the mountain fortress.

"We should stop here and rest until daylight. There is no point trying to sneak in with your—" Reigns motioned toward their faces, "If your tattoos, or whatever, glow as much as you say they do, they will see us coming from a mile away. I think our best bet is to break in during the day."

Will and Sihu agreed.

Taking control of the group, Will said, "Once we have enough daylight, we need to perform reconnaissance. Reigns, do you have any information from your time in the army?"

Reigns rubbed his beard stubble. "I can't say I know much. I never really believed the king existed until a few weeks ago. The fellows in the army always theorized that this is where the coffers were for the emperor. The army was never responsible for its protection. They say some elite force guards it, and from last night we know there is at least one Illkyn there."

"That's not good news. We need information, but first we need some rest. We are going to have a long day tomorrow."

The three slept for a few hours. Since they had approached the mountain fortress from the west, Will scouted the northwest portion, Reigns the south, and Sihu the main entrance from the west. Will and Reigns insisted that Sihu have the shortest assignment due to her recent injuries. Despite her protests and some threats, she eventually accepted.

"Alright," Will said. "We will all be back here no later than an hour before sunset. Remember, don't take unnecessary risks. We already have too much working against us. We still have the element of surprise. Let's keep it that way."

Each of the three went their differing directions.

As Will skirted the northwest side of the mountain, he saw the large fortress off in the distance. Will moved silently, as Fox taught him. The terrain was only slightly different from the forest. He crept from boulder to boulder, from shadow to shadow. Will's mission thus far had been a failure. He procured no useful information and felt as though he only saw a rocky mountainside, not any secret passageways or hidden caves. Will saw outposts at every trail leading up the mountain that could have been used to gain a height advantage. Just as he was about to turn and head back, Will spied a strange sight. He thought it was a delusion and blinked his eyes, but the vegetation was still there. It was the same big, leafy plants Will saw along the river.

A wretched smell came from the greenery. Will fought the urge to turn and run. He had to find out what was happening. There was no excuse to not get information.

Getting closer, Will realized it smelled like his family's outhouse. The ground under Will's feet was damp and the sand seeped water as he stepped. Now into the vegetation, Will saw the source of the sewage: a small pipe with an aged, decaying grate on the end. The grate, presumably to keep out unwanted animals or persons, was rusted badly. Will was sure that the grate could be removed with minimal effort. A few hard, strategic strikes and it could be an entrance. As Will inspected the pipe's potential, he really hoped that the others found another way into the mountain.

Just as Will got up to head back, he heard voices.

"This is the worst patrol of them all. Why do we always get stuck going to the swamp?"

"Because someone has to do it, and because you keep getting on the bad side of the sergeant. If you could just keep your mouth shut, we could take one of the higher patrols."

"Ughh! I think I just stepped in something!"

"We'll just take the long way around. It's not like anything ever happens at this mountain."

Will couldn't believe his luck. The two soldiers had him dead to rights and they simply avoided him for convenience.

The companions gathered at their hovel between two

boulders an hour before sunset.

Sihu reported first. "The only entrance I saw into the main fort is the portcullis. The walls are too high to climb, and a frontal assault would result in our guaranteed deaths. In addition to having boiling tar on the ramparts, there are arrow slits cut into the fortress wall. It is impregnable from the front."

Reigns's report was less detailed. "Stones, patrols, and more stones. I didn't see a single entrance or cave. Only troops on regular patrols."

Will shivered as he thought about what he was going to suggest. "I believe that I found a way in."

"That's great news!" Reigns said, clapping Will on the back. "Where is it?"

"Yeah, Will, that's great! Why do you have that look on your face?"

"The way I found is a small pipe that I believe leads into the fortress. We would have to crawl single file, almost on our stomachs. It is the sewer for the mountain."

The smile left Reigns's face. "You want us to crawl through human waste to get in?"

"It seems to be our safest and least detectable route. The guards who regularly patrol there avoid it due to the smell, and the grate that covers the end of the pipe is rusted enough that we should be able to break through."

Sihu shook her head and shrugged, "This really sounds like the only option, Reigns. Good job thinking outside the box, Will."

"We'll see if you're still thanking him tomorrow." Reigns muttered.

The three continued discussing, trying to think of any other way that they could infiltrate the fortress.

Unable to come up with anything, they decided to break in through the sewage system the next day when the shadows were on the west side of the mountain.

Early in the morning, Will led Reigns and Sihu to the putrid oasis. Once they were sure no mountain guards were in earshot, Will delivered a few swift, precise, kicks to the grate. It broke, leaving jagged, rusty points. Will was the first into the hole. They crawled on all fours. It was not so tight that their stomachs touched, so they straddled the small stream of liquid as they crawled. Reigns had stuffed bunched-up pieces of fabric into their noses before starting their malodorous ascent. This helped with the smell but did not totally alleviate the problem.

After a half an hour, Will saw a purple light ahead. He was grateful that no one in the fortress had decided to seriously use the latrine during their climb through the pipe. Will popped his head up through the opening—a stall in the latrine—and looked around. No one was there. Dim lanterns glowed purple in the room. Rather than producing light by flame, they used stones. While they were not bright, they emanated enough light to see clearly.

Will hoisted himself through the hole and then helped Reigns and Sihu. They took off their wet cloaks and stowed them in a corner. The three used the washbasin to clean off. Once satisfied, Sihu scouted the hall ahead. When the coast was clear, they began their search for the king.

The halls were lit by evenly spaced, purple lanterns. The walls seemed to have been hewn out of a cold-gray stone with streaks of black. Will thought they were beautiful but he knew they had no time to examine them further. The trio moved silently through the halls. Fortunately for the small group, the guards were not so quiet. Due to the vast amount of echoing caused by the cavernous fortress, they always had ample warning before any mountain guards approached. Eventually, the three peered down a small hallway. At the end of the hall was a door with two guards at it. More than this, Will and Sihu could see a hazy-purple wall between the guards and the door. *This must be it,* Will thought.

With a few hand motions, they were all of the same understanding. Sihu took her bow off her back and meticulously unwrapped two arrows, which had fabric around them to keep them silent in the quiver. She removed the arrowheads so that the arrows were blunted. She nocked the first arrow, holding the second ready. Sihu released, and a quick *ting* sung back as the first arrow struck the guard in the helmet right above his eyes. Before the sound of his falling body reached them, another ting sounded, followed by the crashing of the two bodies.

Will, Sihu, and Reigns quickly and quietly made their way down the corridor. Reigns checked the soldiers. Both were unconscious, but alive. The helmets were dented, and small bruises were beginning to form. They hid their bodies the best they could, placing them in the shadows created by the lamps.

Will turned toward the magical barrier. He held his hand out, and as he got close, he felt a tingling sensation. As Will touched the purple barrier he felt heat rushing over his hand, but not burning it. It felt as if the barrier was going around his hand and repelled by it. Will put his second hand through and then pried them apart. To his surprise, a gap appeared in a perfect circle. It got bigger the farther apart his hands spread.

"What's going on?" Reigns whispered to Sihu.

"Will is manipulating the magical barrier. We should go through while he is still able to hold it. Will, is it safe?"

"Yeah, go quickly! It's getting heavier the longer I hold it."

Reigns and Sihu slipped through the hole. Will released the circle and walked through the barrier. It felt as if Will were walking through a wall of hot water.

The last barrier was a door. The guards had no keys on them. As it was designed to keep someone inside, the hinges were on the outside. Using Sihu's black dagger, Reigns worked the hinges until the pins popped out. He pulled, trying to get the door to slip from its frame. Will grabbed the other edge and they heaved together. The door fell off the frame with a solid thud.

Before them lay only darkness. Sihu pried a glowing stone off the wall and shined it into the room. It was not small or large. There was no decoration, only a single chair in the center of the room. And in it, a man was seated. The prisoner opened his eyes when the purple light illuminated the passage. His eyes were gold. Not merely a glowing gold, they burned gold. The golden eyes searched the visitors. A smile crept across the man's face.

# 25

Will, Sihu, and Reigns entered the dark room. The man, the king they had been searching for, stood watching them. Chains fell from him as he rose from the chair. His golden eyes captured Will's gaze first. Instantly, Will felt that the king could see into his very soul. The king was taller than Will had expected, towering over them as he walked closer. He walked with elegance and seemed to cover the distance between them in two strides.

The king, now close enough for Will to make out his features, looked just like the picture Felix showed him. He was strongly built, broad, and athletic. His eyes burned gold, and his face was accented by a well-kept, golden beard, which seemed strange for a prisoner. His golden hair matched his eyes, though it did not glow. If Will hadn't known better, he would not have guessed his age a day older than thirty. His clothes gave away his station in life. Will got the sense that long ago they could have been dignified, but now they were nothing more than shredded rags.

The king spoke, his voice deep but friendly. "Will,

thank you for coming." He paused for a second when the lone lantern illuminated Will's face. "You look just like Macceus. I understand that it has been a difficult journey, but it is best that you have come."

"Thank you, Your Majesty, it has not been easy. This is Reigns and Sihu," Will said, motioning to the other two, who were both kneeling.

The king nodded.

"Will, I have been waiting for your arrival for countless years. You are the heir of Macceus, and you awakened in your race an ability that has not been seen since before the founding of this land."

"What do you mean?" Will asked, confused by the statement.

"When the Valkyns first came about, they did not have physical wings but magical ones. Over time they opted to keep physical wings for reasons of pride, immortality, and elevation of their status among common people. Eventually, they lost the ability to use magic. The ability laid dormant until you came along. It does not surprise me that it was an heir of Macceus to rediscover it."

"I'm sorry, Your Majesty, but I am really nothing special. I can think of a hundred other people more suited for the honor than myself."

"But they are not. You recovered this ability for a reason. Times have changed, and my kingdom will rise again. You are to stand by my side. First, we must free the other Valkyns held captive on the Mount of Fallow."

"Yes, Your Majesty. How are we supposed to do that?"

"Give me your sword, Will."

Will handed the sword to the king.

"Do you know the origins of this sword?"

"I'm sorry, Your Highness, but I do not."

"This sword belonged to Macceus. It was with this sword that he protected our lands against foreign enemies. This sword not only has the power to destroy physical objects, but it has the power to destroy magic as well. You also have this ability to an extent."

Will thought of the mind controlling stone he had destroyed after removing it from Felix.

The king continued, "There is a stone that holds a curse over the mountain. Strike it with the sword and it will release your people."

"Can't I just pull the magic open as I did to get in here?"

"You could, but that would undermine our purpose."

"Our purpose?" Will questioned. He had only sought to free his people.

"Our purpose is to not only free the dormant Valkyns, Will. Our purpose is to free all the land from the emperor. It would be a major blow to the empire if an entire population of rebel Valkyns was suddenly freed, a population they had not known possessed the ability to fight them on their own ground. They would be a beacon of change to the common people and soldiers alike. We will not cower once we decide to reveal ourselves."

"Your Majesty, where is the stone I must break on the mountain, and when will I know it is the proper time?"

"The stone is located at the peak of the Mount of Fallow."

The king picked a rock up off the ground from his dungeon. He pressed the stone between his palms, and it glowed bright red. When he opened his palms, the stone was smooth and red.

"Your magic will not break the emperor's enchantment protecting the area around the stone. You must hold this when walking through his barrier. Once everything is in place, I will tell you when to break the barrier."

"They are just blacksmiths, my king. I don't know how they would stand up against actual trained Illkyns."

"That is true, but we have allies to help train them." The king turned to Sihu. "Sihu, I did not call you here, but I am thankful for your accompaniment of my two allies. I would ask that you would serve the cause of freedom and of the future kingdom."

"I will," she replied.

"I need you to return to your people. I will contact Chief White Lightning. You will accompany those people White Lightning selects to train the Valkyns."

"Yes, Your Majesty."

"Will, you and Sihu will travel together."

"Your Majesty?" Will asked.

"Yes, Will, what is it?"

"What will you be doing during all of this?"

"I will remain here until we are ready. If I escape, we will lose the element of surprise. Additionally, you need time to escape. If I left with you, Lushian would not let you out alive. Rest assured when the time comes, I will walk out of here. And don't worry about the guards you incapacitated. They are my men."

The king walked to where Reigns was kneeling.

"You two may leave." The king motioned Will and Sihu towards the door. "I have business of very sensitive nature to discuss with Reigns."

The two hesitated.

"Go," Reigns said.

Will and Sihu proceeded out of the chamber. Once through the door, they made a point to stand in the shadows out of eyesight of any who might wander by the corridor.

Will asked Sihu, "What do you think that is about?"

"I don't know...We only just met Reigns. The king seems to be honest enough. It must be some sort of secret mission or something."

"What could he want of Reigns that we shouldn't know? He literally just spoke his whole plan in front of all of us."

Sihu responded to Will's growing sense of indignation, "Will, let's not concern ourselves. Our task alone will likely end with us in the ground. In time, I'm sure that whatever is being discussed in there will be revealed in time."

Inside the room, Reigns knelt before the king.

"Reigns...rise. I would prefer to look you in the eyes."

Reigns stood. The king approached him. Now only an arm's length away, the king towered over him. The king gripped Reigns by the shoulders. Reigns's instinct to break away kicked in, but he resisted. As he looked up into the king's eyes, the gold-glowing pupils seemed to swirl. They were mesmerizing, and Reigns lost himself in the swirls.

The king spoke and it broke the trance. "Reigns, do you believe in the cause?"

"Of course, Your Majesty. I wouldn't have abandoned the army and traveled across the empire if I did not."

"Do you trust me, Reigns?"

"Yes, Your Majesty."

There was a long pause, as the king seemed to weigh his answer.

"Reigns." The king stooped and stared directly into his eyes. The king's golden eyes seemed to be molten. "Can I trust you?"

Reigns instantly thought of the less-than-desirable ambush from the emperor. His stomach started to roil, and he thought he might vomit. He tried to look away from the king's gaze but was unable to move. He couldn't run. "I...I...I...," he stammered. "I don't know."

The king cocked his head. "And why is that, Reigns?"

Shame filled Reigns, but right when he was about to confess his run-in with the emperor, the ring on his finger sent a cold chill through his body, as if to warn him.

The king changed his tone to contemplation and said, "What has changed, Reigns? I would not have been able to contact you if I couldn't trust you."

Reigns started to speak, but again the ring hindered him, this time sending a painful pulse through him. Reigns broke his gaze from the king and looked to the ring on his hand.

The king followed his gaze and said, "Ah. What has he promised you, Reigns? Wealth? Land?"

Reigns shook his head. "Essentially," he glanced at

the ring to see how much it would let him reveal. "Life for me until I become useless, but more importantly, life for my family."

The king stepped back and paced back and forth in front of Reigns. One moment Reigns thought he saw anger, the next he thought he saw pity. The king came to an abrupt stop and once again moved toward Reigns.

"I recognize that you are in an impossible situation, Reigns. It seems that you must play a larger role in my plans than I originally intended."

The king shook his head and locked his gaze, as if to peer into Reigns's soul. "You might never see your family again, Reigns. But if you trust me as you say you do, and I believe you do, you must give me their location. You cannot know my plans for them, for obvious reasons. I know you are a very brave man, but what I have planned for you goes beyond sheer bravery."

"Anything, Your Majesty, so long as Elana and Sophie are safe."

"Your role will be that of an informant to the emperor, but you will not reveal all to him. You will enter into his confidence; be warned, he does not trust easily. He will go to tremendous lengths to ensure you will not betray him. You will be tortured beyond anything you can imagine, but once you are in his trust as an agent of his, you will be invaluable to our cause when the revolution starts."

The king went to a corner and removed some parchment and a quill. "Is there any message you would like me to communicate to your family? This will be the last message that you will be able to give to them before this war is over."

"Just tell them that they have all of my love. Everything I do, I do for them... out of love."

"And what must I tell them to ensure them that my carrier is to be trusted?"

"Tell them that, 'When this is over, we will go back to our farm, and live the simple life. I will never again leave them but will spend every day with them until my last breath. That Elana and I will take long walks through the fields, and Sophie can pick as many flowers as we can carry.'"

Tears streamed down Reigns's face.

"Reigns, I'm sorry that this lot has fallen to you, but I see that I can trust you. Here is what you must do..."

Reigns walked out of the chamber.

Will asked, "What was that all about?"

"It was personal...Let's get out of this place."

The three rebels snuck through the dark corridors. Sihu led the group as she seemed to be the only one who was not disoriented by the dark caverns. They entered the small latrine and donned their traveling cloaks and climbed down into the foul drainage system that was their escape from the fortress.

Night had fallen. Darkness and coolness replaced the heat of the desert. The fresh air breathed new life into the travelers. Will breathed in deeply as if he would never breathe air again. *I hope I never have to do that again.* The group traveled to their previous meeting spot.

Will spoke. "We should get an early start. I'll take the first watch as you two rest."

"Sounds good," Sihu said.

Reigns looked distant and pale. "Yeah...that sounds good."

As Will peered across the moonlit desert looking for any abnormal movement, he heard someone stir behind him. He looked back and was aghast. Reigns stood over Sihu with his sword pointed at her chest. Sihu glared up at him wide-eyed.

"Reigns, what are you doing!" Will demanded.

"I'm sorry, Will. I never wanted it to be like this. If you want her to live, you will have to get her to her people quickly."

With that advice, he plunged his sword into Sihu's chest.

"No!" Will shouted, but it was too late.

Sihu contorted as the blade pierced her.

In an instant, Will motioned and was fully transformed into his Valkyn form. He lunged at Reigns with his sword drawn.

Reigns parried with Will for a few moments. His military training was evident as he blocked every one of Will's hacks and slashes.

Reigns shouted over the clang of iron, "Will, I'm sorry, but I have to do this. If you want her to live, you don't have much time! Get out of here! The fortress has to have seen you by now!"

"I hate you! What is wrong with you?"

"Go!"

Will glanced down at Sihu's unconscious body and the pool of blood forming from the wound. Will thought that if he waited much longer, she would die where she lay. It took all of his will to cease fighting Reigns. Will flew back to where Sihu lay. Gathering her in his arms, he took flight. He would not stop until she was safe. And then...he would track Reigns down and kill him for what he had done.

As Will flew, he glanced back to where Reigns had been, but he was gone. The fortress was alive with movement. He flew south toward the Dark Forest. He was surprised at the speed he was able to attain. He crossed over the desert until he spied the Grenvale River. It would be his guide. He kept the Grenvale to his right as he flew south. Sihu's blood drenched his clothes. Though his body ached, he refused to yield to his exhausted muscles.

When the sun was high in the sky, he caught his first glimpse of the Dark Forest. He continued his trajectory, his whole body soaked with sweat and blood. As he approached, Will saw throngs of the empire's troops on the plains bordering the forest. They must have seen him, as two Illkyn sprung from their ranks to cut him off before he reached the forest. Will flew faster, but they were gaining on him. His vision was beginning to blur from the exertion. Will dove toward the edge of the forest, hoping that some of Sihu's people would recognize him. The Illkyn were closing ground, their swords now drawn. He was so close.

*Whiz!* An arrow flew close to Will's face, followed by another, and then another. A whole volley of arrows came from the edge of the forest. He saw one of the Illkyn falling to the ground in an uncontrollable spin. The other pulled up and retreated, as Will landed with a tumble into the undergrowth. In a moment, the people from the tribe surrounded him. He motioned toward Sihu, who he managed to drop before the tumble to the ground.

"Help her! Help Sihu! She is wounded badly."

The next series of events were a blur. He felt someone lift him onto their shoulders. He tried to fight, saying, "Sihu! Get Sihu! Leave me, save her." But it was as if he struggled against a mighty tree. He caught glimpses of the forest moving by as he went in and out of consciousness.

When Will woke, he heard the sound of a gurgling stream nearby. He smelled the smoke of a fire. When he opened his eyes, he saw stars beyond count. Standing over him was the tree that he had struggled against. It was Chief White Lightning. Will tried to speak but his throat was dry. On his second attempt, he was able to say, hardly above a whisper, "Sihu..."

The chief looked down at him. "She will survive. Her wound was not initially serious. However, if she would have lost much more blood, Sihu would not have been able to make it."

# 26

Sihu sat on the bank of the Dark River. The slow-moving waterway ran through the Dark Forest and glowed blue, green, and purple as the colors swirled together. This was the place that she had met Will. She had thought that he was merely an awkward boy who the chief would execute. She felt laughter rise up in her chest as she remembered their first meeting. The rumblings of laughter soon yielded to a sharp pain within her chest. If she had never met Will, she would have never left the forest, her people wouldn't be at war with empire, and she would not have been stabbed through the chest by the traitor Reigns.

Sihu strode down to the water's edge and looked at her reflection. Her black hair was braided over her right shoulder as it always was. Her eyes were a luminous green in the lack of light. Her reflection looked almost as it always did. *What has changed?* She was paler than she could remember. The blood loss had taken its toll. She could not point to anything definitive beside her skin tone. As she looked closer, she saw what it was. She had aged and it was beginning to show. She did not look old, rather her face held that look of hardness that resulted from knowing what a cruel place the world could be.

"What are you doing out here?" asked a voice from behind her.

She would have rounded on the intruder if she had not been expecting him to find her. Instead, her heart fluttered in her chest and she continued to stare into her reflection. She felt his hand on her shoulder before she saw his reflection appear beside hers. She remained silent, leaving his question unanswered. Sihu wanted to reply, but the words would not yield to her will. She stared at his reflection beside her with his arm draped around her. He was tall, with black hair. His face was covered by a trimmed beard that matched the color of his hair. He was muscular, not the boy she originally thought him to be. His most intriguing feature was his blue eyes that shown in the reflection next to her green ones.

"Sihu, what are you doing out here? The people in the camp are growing worried."

Again, she answered his question with silence. She merely reached up and touched the hand that rested on her shoulder. She didn't know why she couldn't respond, but she could not. She sat down and he followed suit. They let their feet dangle in the water and let the colors of the river mesmerize them. After what seemed like hours, she finally spoke.

"Will…"

Will waited in silence for her to continue.

"Will, you saved me. I…I would have died if not for you. Chief White Lightning told me what you did. How they almost killed you while you were carrying me. Why did you risk your life for me? You're too valuable."

"Sihu, I told you after the barracks. I—"

Sihu cut him off. "This was not like the barracks, Will. I should be dead. I had resigned myself to that fact when I felt the steel slip between my ribs. No one should have been able to save me. The chief said he had never seen anyone experience the exhaustion and recovery that you endured upon arriving."

Will was silent for a moment. "Sihu, when you look at your reflection, what do you see?"

"Green eyes, black hair, age… a woman who was once beautiful and strong."

"Do you know what I see, Sihu?"

"Hmm?"

"I see a woman who, of course, exhibits the traits of outer beauty. What sticks out to me is your eyes. They have changed, you know, from when we first met…I remember looking into them and thinking 'this woman is going to kill me.' I thought you were beautiful then, but there was a fierceness that is not there now. There is depth. There is a woman who cares, who loves, and has seen some of the worst this world has to offer. I see the betrayal of a friend that you once trusted."

The words were making Sihu feel sick. The mention of betrayal and of love.

"Sihu?"

Will touched her chin and guided her face until her eyes were looking into his.

"I will never betray you. I would do anything to keep harm from befalling you."

"Will," she said. Tears trickled down her face. "Those are the type of words that are the downfall of men. Reason has to drive us. If not, we will lose this war. We cannot let our emotions get in the way."

"Sihu, this is not about the war. This is about us. I vow, on all that I am, that I will fight for you…I love you."

Sihu's heart felt as if it was torn in two. She wanted to swear to never trust anyone again. Could Will be the exception? If anyone had proven themselves faithful, it was Will. But she had trusted Reigns, and look what that got her. She wanted adventure and it almost killed her. Twice! This was all a result of meeting him.

As she waged her internal debate, she saw Will's eyebrows furrow. He had clearly expected his declaration of love to not lead to silence.

"Will, I don't know why we met. I don't know if it was fate, or destiny, or even if the Eternal King orchestrated it somehow. What I do know is that I have gone halfway through the kingdom, been kidnapped, tortured, and stabbed —"

The furrow on Will's face turned to a frown.

"But, Will, it has been worth it to know you, to love you. I will not trust anyone else, after what I have experienced, and I hope you will be more skeptical of people going forward. But I will trust you. No one else! There will be times in this war that we will be separated, whether from battles, missions, or something else. Do not place yourself needlessly in danger for me. It would break my heart if you died trying to save me."

Will nodded his head, following along. He hugged her close and they sat by the river until the early hours of the morning.

Once back in the camp, Will walked Sihu to her family's tent and ensured she was asleep before he left. The healers told him that she was still weeks away from being able to travel, though she was progressing faster than anticipated.

"She should not be healing so quickly. It is truly amazing that the sword missed all of her vital organs." The healers had said when giving their reports to Will and Chief White Lightning.

Will constantly thought back through the night after meeting with the king. Over and over again, the series of events played out across his mind. He kept coming back to the same question, why? Why had Reigns betrayed them and stabbed her? It had almost seemed that Reigns did it to get them away from that area. Reigns did not seem to desire to kill her, and his judgement was correct. Will was able to get her help in time, if just barely.

"Sir?"

A man of small stature had approached Will. As was always the case with the foresters, however, he moved silently. The whole people group that moved so silently rather unnerved Will.

"Yes, Jax?"

"The chief requires an audience."

"Thank you, Jax. I'll be right over."

Since he returned from the journey to the King's Mountain, the villagers regarded Will with new respect, constantly referring to him as *sir.* The only one who did not address him as such was the chief. Upon asking, the chief informed him that it was because he was the leader of the tribes' strongest allies, the Valkyns. Will thought this humorous as the mountain villagers had no idea what was happening or their potential for the upcoming war. Regardless, he accepted the role and served on the chief's war council.

Will walked into the chief's tent. The husky man was hunched over a wooden table with a hide map spread across it. On the map was drawn the forest and surrounding areas. Placed on it were various figurines, representing the empire's armies. There were no pieces representing the villagers' positions. The chief explained to Will that he would not risk that information being in plain view to prying eyes.

Without looking up from the table, he asked, "How is she?"

"What's that?" Will asked, his mind a little groggy from the lack of sleep the night before.

"Sihu. I heard she snuck out of the camp."

"Oh, yes, of course. She is progressing. She does not need

as much assistance as in previous days. I would be surprised if she wasn't fully recovered sooner than the healers predicted."

"You are likely right. The healers tend to be overly cautious. Unfortunately, war does not allow the luxury of caution."

"What did you need, Chief?"

"Will, as I have told you before, there is no need to call me *Chief.* We hold equal positions of rank. You with the Valkyns, and I with my people."

"Oh yeah, what did you need…White Lightning?"

"I feel as though you have tarried here too long waiting for Sihu to recover. We must act on the king's instruction soon. You need to go prepare your people as best you can. Once my people arrive at the mountain it will not be long before the rebellion breaks out across the land."

"What? I just told you she will only be a few more weeks."

Will knew the argument was frail.

"Will, you are a chief now. You cannot lead by your emotions. You must do what is best for your people. I grow concerned what the empire may do to them if they find out what the king is planning. They may slaughter them all. I would put nothing past the emperor."

"I know what you say is true."

"Sihu will be fine. Isn't that right, Sihu?"

Will turned around and no one was there. A few seconds later, Sihu entered the tent. She was clearly winded from the brief exertion of walking and leaned against one of the posts to catch her breath.

"Will, you need to get to your people and prepare them," she said between breaths. She turned to the chief, "How did you know I was outside?"

"Your breathing was labored. I have to say I am disappointed that you would spy, Sihu."

"Forgive me, Chief, but I wanted to ensure I got to say goodbye to Will. Last time he slipped out of the village before I could," she said, giving him a pointed look.

"You are forgiven, Sihu. I would expect my second to show more integrity."

"Second?" Will asked.

"Yes, once Sihu is well, I plan to split our forces and have half go to your mountain to facilitate training. It should buy us more time. If the whole army is not trying to move at one time, it will be easier to travel unnoticed. That is, unless Sihu rejects the offer."

She simply replied, "I accept," and bowed.

"Will, when do you plan to leave?" the chief asked him.

Will's mouth was still hanging open at the most recent development. "I'll leave by the end of the week. I'll go through the woods and once I'm clear of the empire's scouts, I'll take to the sky."

"That sounds good, Will. We will make sure to send an escort with you until you have your bearings correct," the chief said.

"Anything else you need, White Lightning?"

"Yes, we will need to setup a schedule and a rendezvous in which our messengers will be able to meet you at the barrier of the mountain. Without a schedule, we will not be able to rendezvous and will lose communication."

"That's an excellent point. Who would you like me to schedule it with?"

"Sihu, I believe this is information that we should keep between the three of us. Will, you and Sihu can develop a schedule and a code for interpreting messages."

Sihu and Will spent the next few days together establishing a code and getting supplies. The encampment was nothing like the village they first spent time in. It was not laid out in any sort of pattern. Instead, every dwelling was set up under the cover of trees. Their goal was to avoid detection from the air. Using the unpredictability of the forest growth, no Illkyn would be able to identify their camp.

Sihu and Will walked hand in hand until they came to a small fire outside Sihu's family encampment. Will helped to prop Sihu up, leaning her against a tree. Will sat close by and they talked.

"What do you suppose will happen once the king emerges?" Will asked Sihu.

"Death," Sihu responded simply.

Will changed the subject.

"What about when it's all over? What will you do? When there is no war?"

"I would like to go to the sea. I hear from there, you can see the roundness of the world."

"What is the *sea?* I saw it on my map, but I have never heard of the term. I thought it was some type of plains like the Flat Plains."

"I know very little about it. No living person that I know has ever been there. The legends say that it is an expanse of water so vast that you can see no end. Legends tell us that those who stray out onto it often do not return. Some say those who ventured forth found treasures, while others say they paddled their canoes over the edge of the world. But no one truly knows."

"So, it is like a giant river?"

"Sort of, but much larger. While they say the rivers and creeks sing, the sea dances on the shores."

Will thought of the idea of water dancing on the shores. "I would like to see this sea as well."

"Well… if we are both still alive, we can go together."

# 27

The guards dragged Reigns by his hair, deeper and deeper into their watchtower. The stone stairs bruised his limp body as he drifted in and out of consciousness. The five men tasked with putting him in the cell kept their weapons drawn at all times. Their number had once been seven, but Reigns dispatched two upon being spit on and smacked like a common criminal. He had delivered the message to them that he was there to see the emperor. The men said he was mad and attempted to humiliate him.

When Reigns regained full consciousness, he realized he was not alone, but someone was pulling on his nails. In the dimly lit cell, he made out a host of beady red eyes staring at him. He jerked his hand away from the rats, sat up, and kicked at them. They scampered off, but not to hide. They remained a few lengths away, waiting. A realization hit Reigns. They were not simply waiting for him to die. They were biding their time until he fell asleep again and they could once again feast.

"Don't look at them with such disgust," a raspy voice said from a dark corner. "The rats are our means of survival. Without them we would have nothing to eat in here."

A half-eaten rat leg flew out of the darkness and landed

near Reigns. He looked at it, trying not to retch. It was pink and raw and numerous patches of furry skin still remained on it.

"Who are you?" Reigns asked. His throat was dry and it hurt to speak.

"My name is Meltin. I arrived just a few days ago. I was alone until you showed up, well besides Gilmen." Meltin motioned to a skeleton that had been picked clean. "Apparently the last batch of prisoners got carted off to the pit in Petronev, or they got sent to the slave markets on the coast. Either way, that was a day or two before I got here."

"What are you in here for, Meltin?"

"Disrupting the peace. The slums have been running low on grain and we can't make bread. I went to the upper levels of the cities trying to find wheat, and some rich prick couldn't stand the sight of me. He called the guards and they threw me in here."

"Why is there such a wheat shortage?"

"Apparently, the empire has requisitioned huge loads of crops for the army. Of course, they take from those of us who can't defend ourselves. Enough about me. What's your name and what is your business here?"

"My name is Reigns. I am here because I am seeking an audience with the emperor."

"Why, in all that is good, would you do that?" Shock was evident in Meltin's voice.

"He asked me to…"

"They said you were crazy when they threw you in this hole and now I believe them."

"I'm sorry you think so, Meltin. But for now I would prefer not to talk any longer. My head is killing me."

Reigns's temple was throbbing where a soldier had struck him with the hilt of his sword. Reigns took a few deep breaths, which seemed to help, and assessed his cell. It was square and made of large, rectangular stones. There were no windows. The only light that came in was what leaked around the edge of the door.

Meltin was a young man, but dirty. His clothes were torn and had dark stains. His blonde hair stood out when the light hit it. In contrast, Reigns wore his typical traveling garb. His sword was missing, along with his coin purse and pack, but he still had his traveling cloak which he pulled around him. Reigns finger hurt where they must have tried to remove his ring. He presumed that once the emperor showed up, he would get his other effects back. That is, if the city guard even reported that he had an altercation with them.

Judging by the number of guard rotations, Reigns presumed that he had been in the dank cell for two days. Meltin and he took turns sleeping while the other fended off attacks from the rats. The little beasts were quite practiced, though, and more than once Reigns woke to one chewing on him because it snuck past Meltin's blockade.

The door opened with an abrupt bang. Meltin shrunk back into the shadows. Three guards stumbled in with swords drawn and a torch blazing.

The guard carrying the light shoved it in Reigns's face. "This is the one," he said, as he examined Reigns.

"Oy, get up, filth. We have a game we're going to play with you." The guard snickered as he spoke the words.

Reigns hoped this game was Take Him to the Emperor. Although he was not so optimistic. The men's breath smelled of alcohol and they were too gleeful as they escorted him. No one is ever happy to face the emperor, even if they are merely delivering a prisoner.

They climbed staircase after staircase. After a while, Reigns heard laughing up ahead and the high-pitched sound of someone poorly playing a lyre. The three soldiers prompted him with the tips of their blades toward the room. As Reigns crossed the threshold, he could not believe the lack of discipline. It was a small mess hall with two long tables. There was a blazing fire on one side and a door, presumably to a kitchen, on the other. Men were passed out along the tables and others tried to carry a tune along with the musician. Reigns counted ten in total, including those escorting him. Four were passed out, and the other six seemed to be well on their way. As Reigns entered, the lyre stopped abruptly.

"You!" The man who was holding the instrument stormed across the room. "You killed my cousin!"

He took the lyre and brought it down hard. Reigns turned and the instrument avoided his head, but it broke in two across his back. It was Reigns's instinct to grab the man and fight him to the ground. However, with the amount of alcohol flowing, he liked his chances of getting out of this situation alive.

"Tie him to the chair!" the lyre player yelled.

The men who had escorted Reigns chuckled as they tied him to a chair next to the blazing fire. After securing his wrists and ankles with a thick rope, the men sheathed their swords. The six conscious men surrounded him in a half circle. The lyre player picked up a half-empty bottle of mead and took a swig. Instead of swallowing the spirits, he spit the contents into Reigns's face. Reigns laughed.

"Shut up, you! What? You think you can hurt the guard? I'm gonna cut you nice and slow."

Reigns simply laughed louder. The guards besides the lyre player gave each other concerned looks.

"Maybe we should just take him back to the cell, Cap. He clearly isn't right in the head."

"You will do as I tell you, guardsman, and the only way this pig is going back to that cell is with his entrails on the outside of his body."

The captain pulled a large, serrated and curved knife from a sheath strapped to his ankle.

"You think you're going to scare me with that child's toy?" Reigns continued to laugh.

The captain was no longer laughing or smiling. His face had steadily been growing redder and redder. A large vein pulsated on his forehead.

"You're looking like a strawberry. What's wrong, Captain?" Reigns laughed again.

The captain kicked Reigns directly in the chest, causing the chair to fall backward. He was almost in the fire.

"How do you like that, funny guy? The fire isn't so great is it?" the captain said.

The fire was beginning to burn Reigns's skin. The rope caught on fire on his right wrist. Reigns forced a laugh again. In response, the captain rewarded Reigns with a number of kicks to the chest and face. He put tension on the rope fettering his charred right wrist. It broke free. As the captain was about to deliver another kick, Reigns wrapped his leg with his arm and—pulling the guard over his body—threw the captain into the raging fire. The man dropped his dagger when his body contacted the flames. It fell conveniently next to Reigns. The other men pulled the captain out of the fire as Reigns cut the last of his bonds.

The captain lay steaming on the ground, his body charred. He did not move, except for his chest rising and falling with each breath. The other men paid no attention to Reigns, and he had no desire to kill them. He had to get to the emperor. He began to back away from the group when one of his captors saw him.

"Hey! The prisoner is escaping!"

The guards struggled to draw their swords through their inebriation. During their bungling, Reigns quickly positioned himself between the two long tables. With a table on each side, Reigns could fight his opponents individually, rather than being surrounded.

The first guard lunged and Reigns easily parried and thrust the jagged blade up through his chest. The guard dropped to the ground motionless. In the moment between attacks, Reigns stooped down and picked up the guard's sword. Now wielding two blades, he felt a little more comfortable with one-on-four odds. Of the four men left, three stood before him and one edged around a table to approach him from behind. Reigns quickly engaged the next man and dispatched him with a punch of his hilt to the side of the head. He attacked the next guard, who managed to score a shallow cut on his arm as the two exchanged hacks and slashes. The guard tripped over his fallen comrade, and Reigns brought the dagger down on the man as he fell to the ground.

The man who had separated from the group approached him from behind. There were two left, one on each side. They both held their swords up and approached Reigns.

"Enough!" a dark, cool voice shouted. Reigns saw one of the guards noticeably shutter.

The guards glanced to the door and dropped to their knees. It was the emperor. He was dressed in all black with his hood drawn. Reigns could not make any features out because they were hidden by the hood. The rest of his garb was covered by a dark cloak, though Reigns saw black armor bearing the empire's crest beneath, and a sword strapped to his hip.

The emperor slowly crossed the room. No one said anything, but waited with bated breath for the wraith to speak. The emperor walked over to the captain, who was struggling to breath. With inhuman strength, he simply kicked the man back into the fire. The emperor then produced four red stones from his pocket and placed them on one of the tables. He lightly tapped the table once with his index finger. The stones turned to flames and shot through the air, settling into the chests of each of the men who had slept through the entire sequence of events. They each let out a screech for only a moment before falling limp again.

The emperor approached the four men who remained alive in the room. The one Reigns had hit with his hilt was stirring and, upon realizing who was in the room, struggled to a knee.

The emperor moved without making a sound. He sat down on a bench near the four. "Reigns, sit down while I deal with these three."

The guards looked at each other and gulped. Reigns intentionally sat on the bench opposite the emperor.

"Guards, did you not each swear to follow the Code of the City Guard?"

"Yes, Emperor," they said in almost-inaudible unison.

"What rules have you broken?"

The guards were close to tears now.

"We ain't suppose to be mess'n with the prisoners…"

"That is correct. Prisoners are to remain in their cells until their hearings, or until they are transferred. What else?" the emperor said, raising his voice.

"No drinking on duty."

"Yes. No guard is to be under the influence of any substance while on duty. What is the penalty for breaking these rules?"

"Discharge from service and banishment to the slums," the guard said.

Reigns dared a quick glance at the expanse under the hood. He thought he saw the curl of a smile.

"Good news, my city guards. I am not going to have you discharged. Actually, I am going to promote one of you, since you now see why we have the code." The emperor motioned to Reigns. "Whichever of you is left breathing by the time I leave the room will be promoted to captain. If all three, or even two, are still alive, I will kill you all."

The emperor stood and motioned for Reigns to do the same. He did, and they walked toward the door as the sound of steel striking began. As they reached the threshold only one guard was left.

The emperor looked back and said, "Congratulations, Captain Scenus."

Reigns followed the emperor. He expected the emperor to lead him out of the tower, but instead they went back toward the cells. Eventually they passed the cell harboring Meltin. Reigns grew more concerned. *What does he have in store for me?* They went down as far as they could go in the tower. At the end of a windowless corridor carved from the rock below the city, Reigns saw a singular door. The emperor led him through the door into a room with a chair in the center and a singular, lit, purple lantern hanging from the ceiling.

The emperor motioned for Reigns to sit.

He complied. Cold crept through his body, stemming from the ring on his finger.

"Let's begin," the emperor said.

# 28

It had been a week since Will had left the encampment. Their goodbye flashed across Sihu's mind a few times each day. When the memory came to her, she touched her left cheek, where he kissed her before leaving. She went with him close to the edge of the wood and watched him sneak away through the forest. After only a few moments, he was gone. Sihu wondered if that was the last time she would see him.

"We will look upon the sea together when this is all over," he had said.

"You just stay alive."

"And you," he said with a smile.

He kissed her cheek and then went through the woods.

Sihu was close to fully recovered from her wound. If she ran for too long, deep breaths would cause pain to flare within her. She was glad to be involved again, though she was not often assigned to the patrols. As the second in command of the Dwellers, she and the chief spent most of their time strategizing. One would come up with a plan and the other would attempt to think of all the ways that it would not work. They went back and forth for hours as they evaluated the best strategy to inflict the most damage on the empire's forces while incurring the least casualties.

"Sihu, I think it is time that I reveal what I am thinking," the chief said in a hushed tone.

"I have noticed that we are slowly splitting our forces, but I was waiting for you to give justification," Sihu said.

"I'm glad to hear that. I was testing you to ensure that your emotions for Will have not dulled your reason. You will be commanding battles and you must process events clearly to succeed. You will have to separate emotion from strategy."

"I understand, and it will not be a problem. So, what is this grand plan of yours? I always just figured we were delaying until we retreated to the Mount of Fallow."

"My goal is to keep the majority of the empire's forces here for as long as possible. This will give us time to create a more fortified position than the forest. As you pointed out, we essentially divided our people in half. I will continue to fight with this portion." He placed a small, carved man on the map where one half of the army was stationed. "And you will take this half," he said, placing another representation on the map. "To the Mount of Fallow. Your journey will not be easy, though. In addition to your fighting forces, you will have the children and elderly with you. The cooks prepared enough rations for traveling, but you must be efficient. There will be many perils along the way, and you must be able to adapt. Our scouts created pathways through the swamps so that you can avoid the well-travelled roads. Kihawk and Madoon will guide you, as well as this."

The chief handed Sihu a new map, recently drawn with indications of likely confrontation points with the empire's forces, as well as high and low points. "This map is up-to-date with the empire's movements as of a few days ago. You should be able to go undetected if they stick to these areas."

"And what of you and the others?" Sihu said. "The king instructed us all to go to the Mount of Fallow."

"And we will, Sihu, but we must be smart about our retreat from the forest. I believe we can keep the empire occupied for the coming months, not just weeks. Your half of our force will leave the day after tomorrow, mine will follow in a few weeks. In the meantime, we will not be as aggressive, or rather, we will work to make our presence seem larger than it is. We will burn more fires than necessary, so they believe we have a larger force present. They cannot determine our strength, since we have not met them in open combat. They must judge us by our fires. With your group gone, we will burn just as many fires as we do now. That way, if they find our camp, they will drastically overestimate our numbers. They should have no idea you have left. After a few weeks, my troops will join you at the Mount of Fallow. We will leave behind two dozen warriors who will continue the ruse for as long as possible. We will work to build ready-to-light fires farther and farther back in the forest. That way when the empire pushes, they will feel as though our main force is retreating into the woods, rather than out of it. Once the last fires are burnt and the empire's forces are largely in the forest, our two dozen will work to take out their highest-ranking officers and hopefully Illkyns."

"Who will lead the two dozen?"

"Fox will be our best bet. We will reserve our stealthiest warriors for the task. Although they likely will not survive for long."

"I see," Sihu responded with a hint of sadness, but she understood the strategy behind it. She began to think of all the ways things could go wrong but decided that trickery was their best bet. The empire would chase a phantom army.

"Sihu, once you leave, you must not let any of your traveling party to wander. If word got back to the empire in any capacity, they may push too soon. That means if anyone sees you, they cannot be allowed to report to the empire."

"I understand, Chief."

That night Sihu packed for the coming expedition. The inhabitants of the Dark Forest never travelled heavy. They never had need to, as they existed solely within the limitations of the forest. Sihu had seen the forests of the world beyond their borders and assured the people that their way of life could be sustained. The forests were much like theirs, although quite young in comparison.

The people were instructed to carry some rations, but they would need to supplement them with hunting and trapping along the way. Sihu carried a small pack. In addition, she had a small hammock that could be tied between trees until they found more permanent dwellings. This was the case for all her people. Not only was it easier to travel, but it made tracking them harder, as they would not need to clear campsites. The last thing Sihu prepared was her weapons. She sharpened and oiled her dagger, then waxed her bow string and prepared the quiver.

As Sihu lay in her hammock attempting to sleep, her thoughts drifted to the journey ahead. The weight of her people's survival rested heavily on her. Scenarios played through her mind as sleep slowly found her. She dreamed of the Eternal King. He was proclaiming a message from the center of a dark room. At first his voice was garbled as if he was trying to speak to her from underwater. She moved closer to him and as she did, she realized she was not alone. Will was there. She tried to grab his hand to get his attention, but her hand simply moved through his as if he was made of smoke. She called his name, but he did not respond. He only looked at the king. As she tried to get his attention, he merely stood unfazed by her attempts. In the dream, Sihu was surrounded by people. She recognized Chief White Lightning and the old, portly man, Felix. There was a handful of other people, strangers from varying stages of the social class as evidenced by their clothes. The poorest was a tall, slender man who wielded a trident in his right hand and a net in his left. He had long hair, and a patch covered his left eye. He bore numerous tattoos. There was also a lady, likely in her young forties, as her hair had streaks of gray. Most would consider her beautiful. She bore the face paints that Sihu had to wear while in Fizon and wore more clothes than any other present in the dream. A man that looked to be from Sihu's people was there as well. Oddly, she had never seen him. He appeared ancient. He was covered in tattoos, even his balding head that clung to a few gray, wispy strands of hair.

As Sihu continued to search her dream surroundings, she saw another person she recognized and her heart lurched. It was Reigns. He was the only one not standing at attention. He appeared to be suspended by something she could not see. His presence was not as clearly represented as the others were. He was easy to see through, almost an apparition. Reigns was no longer the towering dark figure standing over her in the night. She almost pitied him. His head hung limply, with his toes barely scraping the ground. Blood dripped down his arms as they chaffed against the shackles she presumed were holding him suspended. Sihu took a few steps closer. As she examined the extent of his condition, she was shocked that he was still alive. She could not check vitals or see breaths, but she presumed he wouldn't be here if he was dead.

"It's sad isn't it?" A deep, smooth voice spoke from behind her.

"It more seems like he is getting what he deserves," she said tersely to the tall, golden-eyed figure staring down at her.

As she looked up into his eyes, now blazing as they bore into her, Sihu recognized that she feared the king. She was not exactly scared, but rather, she saw that he held power that she could not comprehend.

"Why are you here?" the king asked Sihu.

"I was going to ask you that."

"I did not call you, Sihu. You came of your own volition. What is it?"

"Why can't Will hear me?" Sihu asked, rather than answering the question she had no answer for.

The king smiled at her, "Those you see are those who are impeccably loyal to me. They are bonded with me and I with them. After your meeting with me I became bonded with you as well. The others were bonded from birth. It is how I can communicate through dreams. Through our wills, the magic of the land carries and connects us. It only works if both are receptive. I have managed to contact and maintain relationships with all those you see."

"What about him?" She pointed to Reigns, "What is he doing here? He *betrayed* us!"

The king waited a few minutes before responding.

"All those here are loyal to me. Those, like Reigns, who are close to death begin to fade. If he betrayed the cause, why would he be here?"

Sihu was aghast at his comment.

"He stabbed me! How is that not betrayal? Maybe the magic isn't working right."

"Yes, he did stab you, but yet here you stand. You are not dead. Surely a seasoned soldier such as Reigns could have killed you instantly if it was your death he desired. As for the magic, do not dismiss it so quickly. The magic is largely based on potential, and only a few can manipulate it. It is bound by its properties, not by emotion. It cannot be deceived because it has no will of its own."

"You sound like the healers. Regardless, it is not like Reigns stuck around to help out. Will said he took off as soon as we took to the air."

"Your people are very logical, Sihu, but in this you let your emotion cloud your judgement. Not that emotion is bad. In fact, it is necessary to our decision making. The question you're not asking is 'why?' Why did he do what he did?"

Sihu felt the wheels in her head turn as she processed the night's events for what seemed like the hundredth time.

The king broke her from her train of thought. "Look at him. Does it appear he gained some reward for his action, or even that he has been paid?"

"No."

"So, based on the new information, what can you surmise?"

"Well…he stabbed me, but not fatally. The commotion would have drawn the guards to the spot. They would have seen Will take off and lots of blood on the ground… According to you, because he is here, he is still loyal despite his earlier actions, and now he is clearly imprisoned and being tortured. I cannot say I understand."

"Rarely is it good for one to know every aspect, every emotion, every motivation when it comes to a rebellion. Sihu, what you can take away is that Reigns did not intend to kill you."

"I'll never trust him again!"

"Nor should you. It is not bad for our emotions to guide us in addition to our reason. What we can't do is let emotions such as vengeance, anger, or hate infect our internal beings."

"But I do hate him."

"It is my hope that you will not always. He has done things deserving of it, but there were bigger designs at work."

"Did you know he would do this?" Sihu asked, incredulously.

"I knew he would do something. He had to gain the emperor's confidence."

The king strode toward Reigns's hanging body and looked at it. "I just hope he survives the interrogation."

"You did this!" She accused, anger seeping through her usually calm demeanor.

"Sihu, we are inciting rebellion and attempting to overthrow the greatest threat our land has ever known. I have waited hundreds of years for this moment. We must have information about our enemies' movements, but it is not easy to get into his graces."

"So, I shouldn't trust you either?" she scoffed.

"I do not require your trust, but I hope that it can be earned through the coming months and years. I hope all my people will once again have confidence and trust in me as their king. There are times where I must make decisions that others don't. For now, I hope you simply give me the chance to earn your trust going forward."

"You have some work to do," she scoffed

"That I do. You must go now. Your people need to begin moving toward the Mount of Fallow. I am coming soon. Contact me only if absolutely necessary and be ready." The king reached out and touched her forehead. In a split second, she was back in her hammock.

# 29

Will's plan was to sneak through the last stretch of the Dark Forest and into the mountainous swamp he knew from his last trip. From there, he would fly the remainder of the way, hugging the ground and sticking close to the mountains. This would help him avoid detection from the empire. Unfortunately, this plan, as almost all his plans, failed. Will was sneaking through the Dark Forest when the darkness of unconsciousness struck him with a resounding thud.

When he came to, he saw a small ember fire. There were no flames, simply glowing coals with a small spit with a fish on it. Will could not see anything beyond that which the embers and a few magic stones around him illuminated. It appeared that he was in a circular, wooden structure. Through the walls he heard the muffled sound of a gurgling creek.

A voice came from the darkness directly across from him. It was crackled and strained as if the person had not spoken in a long time. "What is a *Fallen* doing in my forest?"

With the question, two narrowed, green eyes appeared across the fire and directed themselves at him. Will tried to sit and found his hands were bound, but not only his hands. Each individual finger was tied to the matching finger of the other hand. He would not be able to transform into his

Valkyn state. This person—he presumed it was a person—knew about his ability to transform.

"What do you want with me?"

*Smack!* Something slapped Will across the face.

"You will respond to my questions with answers, not questions. What is a Fallen doing in my forest?"

Will could not see any form to the being, but he presumed it was human.

"Why isn't there any light? Who are you?"

*Smack! Smack!* Two more quick slaps across Will's face. His cheeks stung, and he thought of an answer to the strange person's question.

"I am trying to leave."

"Trying to leave? You brought all these fires and metal men into my woods and you leave them behind to wreak havoc on us?"

"I…didn't bring them on you."

"Before you came, no metal men or fires touched these lands, and you say that you didn't bring them?"

"They came after me, but I am not their friend. In fact, I am leaving so that I can fight them."

"How can one leave to fight? It makes no sense."

Will was beginning to realize that he might be revealing too much. *This thing could serve the empire.*

"I can't tell you where I am going or my plans, but I promise I intend to fight the 'metal men,' as you call them."

"Then we will wait until you are ready to share."

Will grimaced in the dark. He leaned with his back against the wood, his hands digging uncomfortably into his back. He worked to loosen his bonds to no avail. Will thought it had to be morning, but no glimmer of light entered the hovel. The green eyes watched him, unmoving. As they waited, Will's stomach began to protest his determination. The green eyes moved from Will to the fish over the still-live embers. Will thought he could see an eyebrow raise, perhaps questioning whether or not he was ready to talk.

Will relented. After all, the whole plan hinged on him being able to free the Valkyns. "I am going to free the Valkyns," he said.

"I have seen the Valkyns flying above the metal men. They are not trapped."

"Those are the Illkyn. Their corruption has turned them into—"

*Smack!*

"What was that for?"

*Smack!* The voice came again. "I ask the questions."

Will thought he might strangle the being if he smacked him one more time.

"If I had not met you, I would not have believed that there could be any more Valkyns, at least not blue ones. Where are the blue ones now?"

"They are imprisoned on a mountain. The Mount of Fallow, where Valkynridge use to be."

Will heard what he thought was the tapping of fingers on the dirt.

"This story you tell seems to align with the king from my dreams. What is your name?"

"Will."

In an instant the magic stones, which had only been giving off minimal light, glowed brightly and Will could see his inquisitor. It was a man. Judging by his looks, he had been a Dweller at one point. He was sitting cross-legged, and his hands were making a swirling motion through the air. Will could see that he was balding but had a few scraggly strips of long hair protruding from his head. He stopped his swirling and the room remained lit by the magic stones.

Will started to speak but caught himself in order to avoid another unpleasant smack.

The man snapped his fingers at Will in a whipping motion. Instantaneously, Will's hands were free. As Will began to work the feeling back into his extremities, the old man spoke. "You may now ask questions."

"How did you do that with the stones, and with the restraints?" Will asked in complete awe.

"So, you see the magic, but you don't know how to use it." The old man shook his head with the statement.

In defense, Will said, "I just learned of it a few months ago, and no one has offered to teach me. That, and I have been avoiding drawing the attention of the empire."

"Hmph. Well, we will have to work with you on that. Is that your only question?"

"No! Who are you?"

"I am the Prorok of the inhabitants of this forest."

*I knew it,* Will thought to himself. "I spent a significant amount of time with the Dwellers. They never mentioned you."

"That does not surprise me. I left long ago. The king called to me in my dreams and I listened. They said I was crazy, given over to my old age. They tried to restrict me to my hut, but I escaped. The king told me to wait for the Valkyn named Will, and now I have found you."

"Wait, the Eternal King told you I was coming, and you still went through knocking me out and binding me! Why?"

"The world is at war, Will. We cannot always trust our own perceptions of what we see. We must test and know the truth with our minds as well as our eyes."

Will couldn't believe the words the man spoke. "If the king really did send you and you have spoken with him, what does he look like?"

The Prorok closed his eyes, as if to look back into his memories. "I do not remember the details of his face, as it was in my dreams. I remember eyes that burned like golden embers. I can still see them when I focus. His hair was a matching gold. He was tall and built like a mighty oak. He may look like a man, but he is so much more."

"It seems our experiences have been the same," Will said.

"So then, we are traveling to the Mount of Fallow?"

"We?" Will asked.

"I think his desire is for me to train you and it doesn't sound like you would like to stick around the forest. The king has given us each commands, and the only way we can do both is if I come with you."

"But you cannot fly, and I have to get there as soon as possible."

"You can fly, and I will arrive when I get there."

Will was confused but chose not to question him further. He needed to get moving.

"What is your name?" Will asked, realizing he still didn't know.

The man tapped his chin with his index finger and said in a distant voice, "It seems I have forgotten it. You may call me *Prorok.*"

"What does that mean?"

"It is what I am: a prophet. Here." The man handed Will the fish. "You should eat before we begin our lesson."

After Will had eaten, and drank from his waterskin, the two sat across from each other.

Prorok spoke. "Show me what you can do with the magic you see."

Will formed a small explosive rock.

The Prorok motioned for him to continue.

"That is all I know, and I think I was lucky to discover that. I can also transform into a Valkyn, but I don't know if that is the type of magic you are looking for."

"First, you do not transform into a Valkyn. That is what

you are. That does not change whether or not you have wings. Second, that is different from the magic we use around us. What can you tell me about the magic?"

"It is everywhere, no matter where I go, it seems to persist."

"What else?"

"That is it. Well, the empire uses the magic to surround the Mount of Fallow, and the emperor uses it to control people."

"Well that is not much to go on, so we will start at step one."

Will hung his head a little in disappointment before the Prorok continued.

"The magic particles that you see all around you have always existed in the land. The king and those of a former time merely harnessed the existent power to form the lands. The magic is potential. It is the potential to form, create, and destroy. As it exists everywhere in our lands it is a constant resource that can be used. I have spent my life studying and understanding it. The substance reacts to more than just the physical touch of magical beings. It works with our wills and intentions by using our focus. Your creation of the rocks is the crudest version of utilizing the magic but it is the most common, and quite useful."

Prorok gave Will a demonstration. He waved his hand downward and the room went dark. A moment later he raised his hand and the stones glowed brightly again, illuminating the room.

"Is there something special about the hand motions?" Will asked.

"No. In fact, no two people who utilize the potential will use the same motions. The motions simply help to focus one's will. One could use the potential without motions, but it would be easier to cause something unintentional. You try with illumination. Focus on willing the rocks to dim, focus on their potential to both illuminate and dim, and push them to do your will."

Will sat upright, closed his eyes, and focused his will. He willed that the magic stones would dim. As he did, he motioned with his hands similar to how the Prorok had done. When he opened his eyes, the room was dark. The particles had returned to their normal luminosity.

"Good," Prorok said. "Now illuminate the room."

Will cleared his head, focusing his will. He did the opposite. Before he opened his eyes, he knew he had succeeded.

"Good, good. That should be all for tonight. We will continue tomorrow."

Will wanted to argue but he could feel his cheeks throbbing.

The next morning, Will woke to a slap across the face. He rolled backward and tried to find his sword or the small pouch he kept pre-made stones in. Once he came to his senses, he realized Prorok was standing over him with a small pack shouldered on his gangly body.

"What was that for?" Will asked indignantly.

"You sleep too long. We must be going."

Will rubbed his jaw and said, "You know, it is not appropriate to slap people."

"You are under my tutelage and I will teach you discipline, as you appear to lack it."

Will scowled. "I didn't ask for your help."

"No, but you need it and we both are serving the king in this. It is not your position to ask."

"Fine, but how do you plan to keep up while I am flying?"

"I will meet you at your mountain in a few weeks' time. I have other business to attend to before seeing you again. Don't die."

Prorok handed him a small, sticky pastry. He moved a small piece of bark from the wall, and light streamed through. Prorok got on all fours and climbed out. Will followed him, surprised to find that he had spent the last two days inside a tree.

# 30

Cold water washed over Reigns's face and the cloud of unconsciousness he had been residing in lifted. He attempted to open his eyes. The left was swollen shut but he managed to peek out from under his right eyelid. The king had told him he would endure torture the likes of which he could not imagine. He found this to be a gross understatement. Reigns felt as though every moment of the last week he was on the brink of death. In fact, he had longed for it, but his body and mind never gave him the relief. He had answered the emperor's questions time and time again. Had he met with the king? Why did he stab the girl? Where was his family? What did the king tell him? Where was the boy now?

Reigns had answered truthfully, or at least in half truths. He revealed that he had met with the king through a dream and that he had also contacted Will through a dream. He told the emperor that they were attempting to meet with the king face-to-face. He had stabbed the girl, he said, because he felt his position was being compromised. He gave the exact locations for his family. The emperor did not relent, but continued through the same questions, and Reigns gave the same answers.

As Reigns's grogginess lifted, he realized his hands were

no longer strapped to a chair or hanging from the ceiling. Instead, his body was on the cold, stone floor. He moved his arms. No bonds held him. He moved his legs, and no bonds held them. His breaths felt shallow. He tried to breath the musty air in deeply, but he seemed to choke on it, coughing bloody phlegm. When he finally ceased to cough, he looked around. He saw the departing figure of a guard, a small cup, and a plate of food. He tried to stand and walk, but his muscles were too weak. He settled for crawling on his belly, reminiscent of his early army training. He drank first. The water tasted putrid, but it was wet and it moistened his dry mouth. After draining the goblet, he rested briefly, and then ate the food. It was moldy and smelled rancid. Not even beggars in the street would eat it, but to Reigns at this moment, it was a feast. Upon finishing the meal, he lay on his back and dozed off, his body desperately trying to recover.

The sound of iron on iron woke him as the hinges of the door squeaked to allow a visitor in. Reigns hoped for more water but was disappointed when the dark figure of the emperor entered. He raised his hand and Reigns's body was lifted off the ground and thrust into the chair that had been a bed of torture. Reigns anticipated another grueling session but this time the emperor leaned against the wall and eyed Reigns.

"You have failed me," the emperor said. His voice still sent a chill through Reigns.

He continued, "Fortunately for you, you have not ceased being useful. From what I have been able to ascertain you have been truthful in your answers. Regardless, you did not bring me the boy or help me to deduce much. As a result of your failures, there is widespread murmuring of mutiny within the ranks of my army. They are saying the king is rising. I assure you this is not the case. I have spoken with him and he should pose a problem for us no longer. The boy is isolated with the Dwellers, and I should have them dealt with in weeks. As you know, I do not take mutiny lightly and there is a price that must be paid. I have seen your usefulness in the way you dealt with my city guard. It would be a waste to simply kill you."

Reigns's voice was strained, as it pained him to speak each word. "What do you want from me, my lord?"

"You will be an agent of my wrath against those who seek to betray me. You will weed out those who speak of derision, and we will make an example of them. It has occured to me that I gave you too much freedom when last we spoke. I have ensured we will not have another misunderstanding, or else, it will mean the death of you, Elana, and your precious Sophie. You may notice a few 'modifications' to your body."

Reigns thought he saw a smile beneath the emperor's hood.

"You will not betray me again. You will find it most uncomfortable if you attempt."

"How do you expect me to find out who the traitors are?"

"I have faith that you can do that on your own. Your first assignment will be those who are besieging the Dark Forest. They have made less progress than they should have by now and I suspect the troops besieging the forest of sympathy. You will go and show the general the mark on your forearm. He will give you free reign among the troops. If I do not hear of your progress in this matter rather quickly upon your arrival, you will have served your purpose and I will have no need of you." There was a pause and the emperor shouted, "Jenson!"

The guard hustled in quickly.

"Get our dear friend Reigns his belongings and his horse. He leaves tomorrow."

Reigns left Tizon the following day. The horse he had received was entirely black. The beast was stubborn and took no direction. Reigns suspected that this was due to the black stone embedded between its ears.

Reigns rubbed the back of his hands, both of which now had a dark stone implanted. He recognized them as the same style that Felix had in his back, and as those the horse had. They itched fiercely as the skin around them was attempting to heal itself from their implantation. The last modification the emperor had made to him was a red-and-white tattoo of the empire's crest on his right forearm. It never ceased to glow, though it was less obvious in the daylight.

As he travelled the road, those who saw him shied away from him. Reigns knew they did not see the man who had been a loving father, or a devoted soldier. They merely saw a pale, haunting man riding a terrifying black horse. At first Reigns thought they must have thought him disease-ridden by their reactions, but he soon realized that they feared getting too close to a man they knew was destined for wickedness, and feared the punishment that might be poured out on them if they got in his way.

Numerous times throughout the first day's journey south Reigns tried to draw the horse to a halt so that he could dismount and ease his sore body. The beast refused to yield, and Reigns was imprisoned once again, only this time on the back of a horse. To pass the boredom, he gave the horse a thorough look-over. The stone on its head was not entirely black but emitted a faint red glow from within. He touched it. When he did, electricity arced and shocked his hand. From then on, he left it alone.

"A right pleasant thing, aren't you?" He muttered to the horse. "I think I'll call you Bane because that's what you are to me."

The horse seemed to dislike his new name and snorted in disgust.

"What? What shall I call you then?" He patted the horse's

neck. Glancing at the stone on its head and the ones on his hands, Reigns remembered that it likely had as much freedom in their quest as he had. "Alright, how about," remembering the shock he had received earlier, "Static?"

The horse seemed to nod approvingly. Reigns just shook his head ruefully that his only friend in the world seemed to be a horse whisking him away to a task he was loath to do for an emperor he detested above all others. His thoughts drifted to his family and he hoped beyond hope that the king had saved them and the emperor did not have them, despite his claims.

The sun left the sky and shadow fell over the earth. The stone on Static's neck ceased to glow and he came to a halt. Reigns dismounted and only by keeping his grip on the saddle did he avoid falling to the ground. The horse had stopped in a clearing by the road which seemed to be a regular camping spot, though unoccupied this night. Reigns took the saddle off Static to let him graze. Reigns did not fear him running off because if he did, it would allow Reigns to delay his work for the emperor. Static walked to the small creek that trickled by the clearing and drank before grazing.

Reigns gathered a small amount of dry wood and started a fire. He drank from his water skin and refilled it at the creek. He lay down by the smoldering ashes with his head resting on the saddle. As sleep found him, Static lay down beside him. Reigns slept deeply, fearing nothing, as death would surely be a relief to his current plight.

He dreamt of the small torture chamber that had been his room for innumerable days. In his dream, he paced in the cell until the emperor entered. The emperor knocked him over and dragged him by the foot around the rocky cell. It seemed odd but despite all he did, the emperor would not stop. Finally, he awoke to see the long, dark face of an animal dragging him across the ground. He kicked his leg and the animal released him. The sun was just coming up over the clearing, and the animal was Static. The stone was once again emitting its red glow from between the horse's ears. Reigns grumbled as the horse directed him toward the saddle. The horse, willingly or not, was apparently responsible for ensuring his cooperation. He saddled the beast and mounted. Once again, they were off.

As the day turned from afternoon to evening, the saddle soreness Reigns experienced became nearly unbearable. He shifted positions every few minutes. During one such time, a black streak flashed across his vision about three feet in front of him, followed by sharp thud as an arrow buried itself in the tree just to his left. The horse reared at the unexpected projectile and due to Reigns's shifting, he fell from the saddle onto the worn road.

He rolled toward the woods opposite where the projectile had come from. There he waited, listening and glancing from the berm in an attempt to identify the attacker. Static, rather than fleeing from the initial disturbance and subsequent fall, charged headlong into the opposite side of the woods. Reigns had heard of horses trained to fight in combat and was now gaining a new respect for his guardian and traveling companion.

After about an hour, Static returned to the road and seemed to be at ease. It trotted up beside Reigns, waiting for him to mount. Reigns, trusting that the beast had either eliminated the threat or driven it far enough away, crawled from his hiding place. As he placed his hand on Static's saddle to pull himself up, he glanced at the arrow. There was something strange.

Reigns made for the arrow, but Static blocked his path, attempting to force him back in the saddle. "I'm not going anywhere, Static. It would irresponsible of us not to examine the projectile. I think that is what our overlords would want. We should try and find out who is attacking us." These words seemed to appease Static, especially in light of the fact that they were not running from their intended purposes.

Reigns approached the arrow, which had yellow fletching. As he got closer, he was able to identify the peculiarity. There was a parchment wrapped around the shaft and tied with string. Reigns reached up and dislodged the arrow. As he cradled the dart in his hand, he untied the string and slowly unrolled the parchment. A small, dried, and half-crushed flower fell out and onto the ground. Reigns scooped it up quickly and turned his attention back to the parchment. There was only one word written on it: "Safe."

# 31

Will approached the mountain that up until the previous few months had been his home. It was dark now and the deep purple curtain that enveloped the mount stood ominously before him. *Not for long,* he thought. His people had been restrained to this place for centuries. Soon they would be serving the king in a righteous rebellion to overthrow the empire. He reached in and peeled the curtain apart and stepped through. The air was heavier than what he had breathed during his previous weeks and months of travel.

Will made his way up the mountain, eventually reaching the familiar terrain of his childhood adventures. He snuck through the darkness that was only illuminated by the magical dust that he had never seen until the night of his ceremony. He thought back to that night, to the whispers and murmurs of the crowd. He thought of his father, Merle. His father had looked on him, not only with pride, but with hope. The tearful farewell he bid his dad replayed through his head. *Will I see him? What did the empire do to the people of Rand when I left?* The thought was one that had plagued him frequently in his travels. He resolved that he would not think of it until his return.

Fears arose in his heart. He thought of the terrible things

the empire did to Felix. He imagined his father, his mother, and his brother in their torturous grasp. He blinked small tears from his eyes. *What did I do to them?* He stopped to catch his breath. The village was over the next ridge. *No. I did not choose this. I was chosen by the king, and the people of Rand sent me out and now I am returning, and they will be freed.*

Will snuck to the top of the hill and peered out. The sight of the town he had always loved disturbed him. The once-peaceful village was surrounded by a wood-beam fence. The wall was made of interlaced horizontal logs with sentry fires posted every thirty to forty feet. Will decided it would be best to circle higher up on the mountain to get a better look at what was happening in the village. He knew of a vantage point where he should be able to fully observe the inside of the village. Utilizing the cover of darkness, he snuck unseen around the city and up the mountain, high enough to see over the newly constructed barricade. As he slid into the cover of a small grove of pine trees, the sun was rising over the mountains.

Looking down into the village of about two hundred homes, Will immediately noticed that his childhood home was reduced to ashes. Along with his home, several other buildings had been visited by the flames of punishment: namely, the food warehouses, a few houses besides his own, and the village hall. The destruction was not all that had entered the village of Rand in his absence. There were a number of new crudely constructed structures. Anger burned within Will as he saw that the most prominent of these was a pair of stocks and a whipping post in the town's center.

Will seethed, but he forced himself to detach from his emotions and think clearly. *There is no way I can do this on my own. I will have to wait for the reinforcements from the Dark Woods.* Will decided that he would busy himself with observation until the reinforcements showed up in a week.

He could not risk contacting anyone in the village, lest he give himself away needlessly. But if the opportunity presented itself to talk to his father or the chief, he might not be able to resist.

The week of Will's observations provided valuable insights into how the village was currently operating. Rand was now under the direct rule of an Illkyn who presided mainly from a large, walled tent. It only left the tent in order to perform regular inspections and to punish the company of troops which now ran the village. The troops were the most disciplined troops Will had yet seen. They were constantly vigilant, and Will was unable to catch any falling asleep on duty. As he looked for weaknesses in the defense, or the weak soldier he could exploit, he was continually let down. Will presumed this was a result of the Illkyn's delight in shaming and punishing his own men. After Will saw the Illkyn, he covered his tattoos in mud to avoid revealing himself.

The villagers were nothing more than slaves under the new regime. A bell tolled early in the morning and all those able to work the smithies marched from their houses to the forges. Will had not seen a single straggler, which seemed strange as there was a number of older men who lived in the village. Will only caught fleeting glimpses of kids or the women who did not work the forge. Occasionally they would tend the gardens under strict supervision.

What was most concerning for Will was that he did not catch a single glimpse of his father or any member of his immediate family. With such a closed community, Will was related to many of the villagers and saw a few cousins, uncles, and aunts. His mother, father, and brother, however, avoided his detection.

During the week, Will made one trip down the mountain to meet with a messenger of the Dark Forest. He scribbled down his report and sent the messenger on his way.

Three weeks later, Will made his way down the mountain and waited just outside the mountain's curtain barrier for Sihu and her reinforcements. His mind rushed with the possibilities and outcomes of where, when, and how they would free the village. He knew that of the hundreds of scenarios plaguing his conscious that the outcome would likely be something he had not thought of, and that he should stop worrying about it. Despite all his doubts and role-playing, it was certain that people would die and that he would be responsible to fight the Illkyn.

After waiting a few days, Will began to doubt whether the Dwellers survived the journey. As the sun set on the third day, he was cooking a small jackrabbit on a low fire. As he turned it for the last time, he heard a voice directly behind him.

"Hello Angel."

Will turned to see Sihu's deep green eyes. He hugged her, pulling her close. As the moment dragged on, she started to take a step back, but Will did not yield. She simply hugged him back, waiting for him to release her.

"How are you doing? I feel as though it has been ages since I have seen you." He held her cheek lightly with his hand.

"I am doing quite well. I am healed and stronger than ever. How was your journey? You are looking thin."

"Well, that is a more difficult answer. First, before we talk about me," he looked over her shoulder into the darkness, "Where are the reinforcements?"

"They are a few hours away. The scouts told me where you were, and I thought it would be best for us to talk alone before we had an entire camp with us. Now tell me what is going on."

"Rand has been taken over by a company of the empire's

soldiers. They are led by a particularly vicious Illkyn. There is no way I could have taken them on by myself, so I have been sticking to observation until we could mount a full attack."

"I see. Do you have an exact count?"

"From what I have been able to gather, their numbers are between one hundred and one twenty-five. They are well-trained and disciplined to the man."

A look of concern shot across Sihu's face. "What of your family? Were you able to find out what happened to them?"

Will looked away from Sihu, fear rose up inside him, but he forced it back down. "I have not seen any of my family. I have not even seen the chief. The hut which I grew up in was burned to ashes."

"I'm sorry, Will," she said, placing her hand on his.

She changed the subject back to the assault. "I will go with you in the morning to scout the area again and then we can make our plan of attack."

"When will Chief White Lightening and the others get here?"

"He will not be coming for a few more weeks. We had to split our forces in order to keep the armies of the empire occupied and avoid being pursued."

"So how many people are coming?"

"I have with me a total of one hundred and seventy-four, of those one hundred and thirty should be able to fight."

The news was a hard blow to Will's many mental simulations of certain victory. Strategy would now come more into play than Will had previously thought.

"Should we try and contact the villagers?" Will asked.

"No, I don't think that would be best. Right now, our most significant advantage is in the element of surprise. They don't know we can get onto the mountain. My guess is that the whole company and the Illkyn are here to fight you when you arrive. If they had thought you would be bringing a force of your own, they would have stationed a battalion."

"We don't have your chief, we are about to face a company of at least one hundred and twenty-five soldiers in a heavily fortified position with only a slight numbers advantage, and I have to fight a highly trained Illkyn. Is there anything else?"

There was a brief pause in the conversation.

"I have spoken to the king in my dreams. It seems I have a more direct connection to him than most people he has contacted. My guess is that it stems from my close call with death, but I am not sure. He says that Reigns is still loyal to him. That what he did to me was in order to be planted as a spy in the emperor's confidence."

"That's insane! How could the king do that?"

"The king said he did not know exactly what Reigns was going to do, but he understands why he did it and asked me to do the same."

Will felt his heart pumping rapidly and his blood pressure rise.

"Is there anything else our king said?"

"Yes. The rebellion will start one week from today. We must free your people as soon as possible and begin training them. There is no good way of telling how long we will have before the empire discovers the ruse being played on them in the Dark Forest or that we are going to free the Valkyns."

Will calmed down as he remembered the grand scope of the conspiracy. He could not trust Reigns again, but he now had more clarity and answers about the night that had haunted him.

The two sat and talked the remaining few hours before the forest dwellers began to trickle in. Will thought it strange that they did not march in columns, but quickly realized how they had been able to avoid detection by sneaking in a disordered unit through the foothills of the mountains.

Sihu eventually strung her hammock and laid down as

Will slept on the ground close by.

Will and Sihu woke early the following morning. Will held the barrier open and they passed through as the sun began to crest over the mountains. They worked their way up the difficult terrain only stopping for a quick bite to eat and to rehydrate from their waterskins.

As they approached the village, they made quick surveys of the landscapes from each potential attack position. Sihu recorded brief notes pertaining to the landscape and strategic positions. They spent the remainder of the day assessing the troops and their armor, discussing the weak points that archers could exploit. The guards wore full plate armor with helms. The only weak points would be under the arms, behind the knees, or the neck which, at times, was exposed if the soldier faced away.

Once again, the Illkyn only appeared to execute punishment. A soldier was late for his shift and was whipped nine times. Will tried to perceive any weakness this Illkyn might have. He was like the others Will had seen. His face was deformed by jagged scars, small horns protruded around the crowd of his head, and his tattoos, which were visible during the day, lacked any of the symmetry that Will's had. His face looked as if it had been consumed by chaos. The beast smiled with glee as he punished the soldier. As the man screamed it was evident that he would not be fighting in the upcoming assault. Upon finishing the punishment, the Illkyn stalked back to his tent.

Will and Sihu gathered all that they needed to organize a proper attack and made their way back down the mountain.

# 32

It was dusk as Will approached the barrier surrounding the village of Rand. Attached to his left arm was a large shield and in his left hand he held a magic stone. Up to this point he had made his way forward slowly and meticulously, but now was the time to reveal himself. He took a glance around to try and see Sihu or any of the Dwellers. He should have known better. They seemed to have the ability to vanish into their surroundings at will. *This has to be the stupidest thing I have ever done,* Will thought. *Or the bravest.*

He pulled his arm back and threw the stone with all his strength. There was a loud *boom* and a gap appeared in the barrier. Within moments, imperial soldiers were shouting to one another and preparing to defend against the attack. Will ducked behind the large shield as a volley of arrows rained down around him. He launched another stone and the soldiers realigned themselves to the best defensive positions as their barrier began to burn.

*"Halt!"* a voice shouted from within Rand.

The soldiers ducked out of view and seemed to wait. The first part of the Illkyn that Will saw was his eyes as he walked through the dark smoke rising from the wall. The beast strutted out of one of the openings Will had created. Despite his yelling, he did not look angry. Rather, a smirk passed over his purple lips.

"Who goes there?" he asked in a calm demeanor.

"I am Will, son of Merle, and a villager of Rand. Yet, I do not recognize you or your men."

"Recognize me? I am your lord, boy. All those from Rand serve me, and through me, the emperor. But you, you will serve the emperor, just not here."

"You must be delusional if you think you are anything but the lowest of low in the empire. You are a slave. You think you have power, but you are more captive than any person you think is below you."

Will seemed to have struck a nerve.

"Enough!" the Illkyn shouted vehemently. "Why do you hide yourself? I have heard the reports. You travel as a man but are a Valkyn."

Will gestured with his hands and his wings appeared. This state of being was beginning to feel more natural. Will drew his sword.

"Won't you be diplomatic about this? It would look better for all of us if we took you alive," the Illkyn responded.

Will raised his sword in an attack-ready stance. "I would never go willingly with an Illkyn."

At the mention of the word *Illkyn*, the beast fumed. His tattoos seemed to pulse a brighter red.

"The emperor said he preferred you alive, but he would take you dead just the same!" The Illkyn turned sideways to the men now mostly gathered at the wall. "On me! If he gives us too much trouble, fill him with arrows."

The Illkyn stalked towards Will, who had been slowly working his way backward during the brief interaction. The Illkyn was followed by what Will guessed were two groups of twenty troops. As they got close to Will, they fanned out, surrounding him in a circle of bows and swords.

"Face it, child, you can't run. If you try to fly, we will shoot you out of the air, and if you get away, I will come for you. It was foolish of you to show yourself here."

"You call me the fool, but you and your emperor are the fools! The Eternal King lives and he is ready. You kept a small army of Valkyns imprisoned for hundreds of years. Luckily for me, you are the fool and will not live to see the rebellion!" Will spat.

With the word *rebellion,* soldiers all around them began to drop to the ground with arrows protruding from their necks.

"It's a trap!" a soldier shouted just before he fell to the ground.

The men scrambled for cover. Will attempted to take advantage of the chaos and charged the Illkyn. The Illkyn turned and easily deflected Will's attack. As Will recovered from the swing, the Illkyn leapt in the air, gaining height with each progressive flap of his red wings. Will knew he couldn't let the Illkyn get the height advantage. He leapt after him and ascended, trying always to stay behind him so the Illkyn couldn't attack him. Once they were a hundred feet above the chaos below, the Illkyn, who had outpaced Will, turned and dove at the still-ascending Will. His sword glowed blood-red and was directed at Will as the beast dove toward him. Will, anticipating the stab, moved to parry. At the last moment before contact, the Illkyn opened its wings, creating drag which allowed him to alter his attack from a stab. He dodged Will's parry and sliced down the length of Will's torso. Will's padded-leather armor split from the attack and Will felt the warmth of his blood moistening his undershirt. Leather armor was useless against this sword. The cut was not deep but it was long. He couldn't draw this out or he would pass out from blood loss.

Now at equal height, the two circled each other as they exchanged blows. Neither would allow the other the other to move into a higher position. It quickly became evident that the Illkyn was the superior swordsman and practiced in aerial combat. Will briefly glanced around, looking for anything to gain an advantage. There was nothing. Will was totally at the mercy of the Illkyn, high in the sky and far from help.

As Sihu watched the trap spring, she was proud of her people and the efficiency with which they dispatched forty well-trained and armored military personnel. Once the last of the men was taken care of, she turned her attention toward the village. She desired to watch the blue and red figures dashing above, exchanging blows with magical weapons. It looked as if fire and ice were fighting high above them. She looked once and caught her gaze lingering. She could not afford to lose focus.

Sihu whistled three times and the Dwellers disappeared behind their cover. The men behind the barricade tried to use arrows to take care of the Dweller's threat. Unfortunately for the imperial soldiers, their trap sprung right outside of bow range and the smoke of the burning barricade cut down their ability to see.

A small Dweller appeared beside Sihu. "Report," she commanded.

"The villagers are willing to fight. Basen's group is in position."

"Excellent. Give the signal."

The small Dweller known as Deder sprinted away. A moment later, a torch was lit from the direction he had run. It burned brightly and screams emitted from the barricade. Basen's group of archers had snuck above Rand while all attention was focused on Will and the trap. Basen's group rained arrows down over the barricades. Sihu led her group slowly toward the burning barricades. The smoke was so thick now that no one could see past the wall. Sihu sparked some steel and flint she was carrying, twice. A short distance off, Deder lit another torch and the volley of arrows stopped raining down.

The Dwellers moved with efficiency and stealth through the village, eliminating the remnants of the soldier's men. After a few minutes, Sihu heard the battle cries of men and the clanging of steel. This was not the sound of the Dwellers fighting. No, this was the people of Rand fighting against the soldiers with blacksmith hammers and commandeered swords.

After another few minutes, the fighting in the village was over. Basen approached Sihu.

"Are all the enemies eliminated?" Sihu asked.

"We are going from house to house to ensure we have no issues. The sweep should be complete in a few hours. What of our Valkyn?"

Sihu looked up as fire and ice circled each other high above them. "It appears our Valkyn is hurt. He might not be able to last much longer…"

Basen looked up as well. It was clear to any trained fighter that Will was outmatched, and his movements were becoming slower.

"Basen! Go gather your archers and send for Deder. I have an idea."

Basen ran, and was back in a minute with eight archers. Deder brought up the rear.

"Deder, implement the mountain defense. You nine, with me," she said, motioning for the archers to follow her back outside of the village.

With that, they moved out of Rand. Sihu grabbed a piece of the burning barricade as they left.

Indeed, Will was losing ground quickly. He lost more blood

and his vision began to blur. As he rotated around the Illkyn, something on the ground caught his attention. Someone was waving a torch in a circular pattern and it gave Will the faintest glimmer of hope. Their attack must have worked, and now he needed them to help him. Will disengaged the Illkyn and did an aerial dive. Tucking his wings around him, he dropped like a star falling from the heavens. The Illkyn dove after him.

The cold mountain air swept across Will's face as he plunged toward the ground. His eyes began to water. The torch stopped spinning and he was approaching quickly. Too quickly. Will deployed his wings, but he had misjudged. They slowed him down, but his momentum still carried him hard into the ground. He attempted to roll, but the impact was too strong for any semblance of a controlled roll. He crashed hard into the ground and heard a loud snap. Pain shot up from all around his body. He was on his back, his chest vulnerable to the Illkyn who descended toward him, sword ready to strike. He slowed his descent but not so slow that Will would have time to block his attack.

Will caught the face of the beast in his gaze. Nothing burned behind his eyes but hate and anger. Killing Will was clearly not a conflict of interest. Will wondered how many Valkyns he had killed before. As Will accepted his fate, the look on the Illkyn's face changed. It no longer held hate and anger. For that matter, his eyes no longer burned red at all. They turned a cold gray. Multiple arrows had just ripped into the Illkyn's chest. The beast's wings caught the wind and beat erratically as he plummeted toward the ground, landing with a loud crunch right next to Will. The red sword flew out of his hand, clanging harmlessly a few paces away, as its wielder impacted the unforgiving earth.

Sihu was the first to reach Will. Upon seeing the gash that ran the length of his chest, she immediately called for two warriors to move him inside and get one of the healers. He was their main priority. Will faded in and out of consciousness as they carried him toward the village.

When Will came to, he felt as if each breath was trying to rip the skin on his chest apart. He opened his eyes and saw the familiar thatched roof that was so common in Rand. As he looked around the room, he recognized the layout, but did not know whose house he was in. Beside him, he saw Sihu. She had fallen asleep with his hand wrapped in hers. He did not want to wake her, but he decided to let her know he was alright.

Will squeezed her hand gently and spoke, "Sihu, wake up."

Sihu startled awake, snatching her hand away and looking for an attacker.

"Sihu, it's just me."

The tenseness left her body and she looked at him.

"I'm glad to see you awake. For a while there, we weren't sure you were going to make it. You had quite the fall, and if that gash on your chest was any deeper it would have been fatal. The healer couldn't believe that you fought for so long with such a wound."

The scenes of the battle came rushing back through his mind and he lifted up the sheet to look at his chest. The effort caused pain across the fresh wound but nothing unbearable. He looked down and saw stitching down the entire length of his chest and onto his stomach.

Placing the sheet back down he asked, "How long have I been out?"

"Three days."

"What of the people of Rand? How many survived?"

Sihu looked away from him, clearly not wanting to say anything.

When she spoke, she said, "We lost only nine of the villagers during the battle. For the most part, the element of surprise played heavily in our favor. We lost twenty of my people in the attack."

"And what of my family? Have you heard anything?"

She looked at the same spot on the floor away from him, "Will..."

"Just tell me... please," he implored.

"The company of soldiers came a month after you left. From what I have gathered from the villagers, your father sent your mother and brother away the moment they showed up. He was preparing for something. Sadly, he stayed behind to give your mother and brother more time. They tortured and killed him within the first few days."

Hearing the words felt like a kick to the stomach.

Will stuttered, "A...any word of my mother and brother?"

Sihu hesitated again. "The Illkyn stationed here was relentless in trying to find them. About two months ago, one of their patrols came back with your mother. The people say the Illkyn made an example of her for those who would attempt to run away. I'm so sorry, Will."

"What of my brother?"

"No one knows. He could be out there, or they could have killed him taking your mother. No one had the nerve to ask the soldiers."

Hope. Sihu had just given Will hope that not all of his family had died. He would need to search for him. He knew all their old hiding places. But first he would need to organize the village. If his brother was alive, he would be able to survive a while longer, especially with the threat of the empire eliminated.

"Sihu, can you have all of the elders and the chief meet me here? I need to talk to them."

"They are all dead. Anyone who had any role of leadership

was killed upon the imperial troops' arrival. From what I can tell, the village is looking to you to be their leader now."

Will groaned audibly. He was not sure he wanted to command an entire village of Valkyns.

"Alright, could you gather everyone in the square? I need to speak to them."

"Yes. There is one more thing you must know."

Will waited for her to continue.

"The king and I spoke in my dreams last night. I informed him of our victory. He told me that he has to break free within the week. The emperor caught on to some of his plans and he needs to give the people their symbol to rally around. The rebellion is about to start. He asked that we fortify the mountain and as soon as the rebellion starts, to remove the veil so people can come in. This mountain will act as a base for the rebellion. He will be coming here."

"How will we know when the rebellion officially starts?"

"He did not give details, just that we would know."

"Let's gather the villagers."

Sihu stood and stooped over him, kissing him on the forehead. As she withdrew, he reached up to stop her. They stared at each other for heartbeats, and then he kissed her lips. The pain in his chest eventually forced him to rest back in the bed. She winked at him and left the room.

Once all the villagers had gathered around, Will spoke. "The empire has exploited our people for too long! They took our freedom and many of those we loved. I was appalled to hear of the murders of my father and mother, Chief Boxfen, and the elders. They were savagely cut down by an empire that kept our people imprisoned on this mountain for centuries. Today, we no longer serve the empire. The Eternal King lives! I have seen and spoken with him. Our history goes deeper than any of us thought. Our people once fought side by side against evil when it swept across this land, and we will once again stand against it. We will take our rightful place beside the king, fighting the evil that infests our land."

As Will finished speaking, he gestured, and his wings appeared. The people stood gaping at him.

"We are Valkyns! I was commissioned by the king to release you from your bondage and train you. Our cause is just, and I implore you to join us. Know this, the king will not force you to serve him, but he will accept your fealty voluntarily through me. Come, let me remove the shackles that have held you for so long."

The crowd cheered and formed a disorderly line before Will. With each person that came forward, he simply gripped their shackles and broke them off by prying with his hands. They took oaths of fealty to the King as their shackles dropped to the ground. Only a few older people rejected taking the oath, and parents kept those too young to recognize the implications of such an oath from taking them. Besides that, Will was tasked with training hundreds of Valkyns. Will thought they had a formidable group, though he did not know how many Illkyn existed under the emperor's control.

"You begin training in two days. Tomorrow, we'll shore up the defenses. Listen to the Dwellers. They are our closest allies and came here to train us and establish a stronghold on this mountain. Each day we will build defenses and train for combat."

Another cheer went up and Will left the square, followed closely by Sihu.

Once back inside the home, which Will learned had previously belonged to Chief Boxfen, he planned with Sihu.

"What is the plan tomorrow, if not training?" Sihu inquired.

"We go to the top of this mountain and wait for the

rebellion to start. Then we destroy this curtain per the king's instruction."

"Excellent. I will send one of my men down to wait by the veil to guide our remaining people up. Chief White Lightning should be here within a week. Until then, I will have Basen establish the defenses and send my scouts to watch the paths and roads where we will be susceptible to unwanted visitors once the mountain's barrier is lifted."

With a little too much enthusiasm, Will said, "This mountain will be defendable in no time!"

"The mountain is only defendable if the Valkyns can fight in the air. We will be at the mercy of the Illkyn until then," Sihu corrected him.

"We will have a couple days to journey to the top which should be about the time we are to destroy the veil. In the meantime, we cannot afford to wait to train the people Rand. Could you designate someone to start training the Valkyns with the sword?"

"Yes, I'll take care of it before we leave tomorrow morning."

"Any chance you brought Thunk?"

"Unfortunately, no. He opted to remain behind and fight the imperial forces in the Dark Forest."

Will missed Thunk. He winced, remembering his own training. On second thought, the villagers of Rand were probably luck.

# 33

After two days of hiking, Will and Sihu made it to the peak of the mountain. Will had anticipated a difficult journey but, aside from his healing wound, it was not too trying. The months of hiking through the land had paid off and his muscles and endurance were stronger than they ever had been.

Will had never been to the peak of the mountain before. The kids all stopped when the snow got too deep to travel. Will and Sihu fashioned snowshoes to continue hiking. It was a half a day's walk on the snow to the peak. On the ridge line, cresting the top of the mountain, the wind blew snow around them as the sun dipped below the horizon. Will and Sihu saw the place where the veil emanated, a short walk away from the ridge. There was a small platform of rocks shaped in a pinnacle with a large, purple gemstone resting on top. From there, the veil radiated outward. Surrounding the pinnacle was a thick wall of red substance. It seemed to have the viscosity of water as they looked through it.

"I guess we wait until the king contacts us," Will said.

The two found a large boulder to block the wind as they waited. They scraped together some dry wood and made a small fire to keep themselves warm. Will and Sihu sat holding each other and looking out over the world below. The veil, and the air closer to the top of the mountain, seemed thinner. They were able to identify the Flat Plains far below, but cloud cover hid most of the other features.

When the moon was high in the sky and Sihu was asleep, her head resting on Will's shoulder, there was an immense explosion off in the distance. It emanated from somewhere Will could not see. A moment later, a continuous ray of golden light shot into the sky. Sihu sat up quickly and drew her knife at the sound of the disturbance. The two sat memorized by the pillar of golden light. After they stared for at least a half-mark, it suddenly ceased.

"I guess that was him," Sihu said.

"Let's do this and get back to the village."

Will pulled the stone the king had given him out of his pack and his sword from its scabbard. Holding the smooth, red stone in his left hand, and his sword in his right, he walked toward the liquid-like barrier. As he approached, Sihu grabbed his shoulder, holding him back a moment, and kissed him.

"Hide behind the boulder until this is destroyed. Who knows what will happen when I strike it?" Will said. Concern for Sihu was evident in his voice.

She hugged him and moved back to the boulder.

Will entered the substance and approached the pinnacle. The red substance filled his lungs and began to burn. Will felt the stone in his hand pulse and the burning subsided. As soon as he was in range, Will swung a massive overhand strike at the purple gemstone. Upon impact, the sword sent a vibration through Will's arm and body. He just managed to hang on to the sword. The gem began to crack and fissure. Will saw a bright light like the sun from within as the stone cracked around it. He turned and ran, diving behind the boulder next to Sihu. A moment later an explosion rocked the mountaintop. Will looked around. The veil was cracked and parts of it were slowly disintegrating and turning into dust, dropping to the ground below. He peered around the rock and the pinnacle was completely gone. As he stood to inspect the spot of the explosion, he saw that the boulder they had been hidden behind was charred from the blast.

Sihu and Will gathered their small packs. The veil was almost completely gone, and the air felt fresh for the first time since they entered the veil. They began the descent hand-in-hand.

Will felt a sense of satisfaction as they travelled down the slopes. He had accomplished what he set out to do. His people were free, no longer slaves to an evil emperor. But he knew his adventure was just beginning.

# 34

## Epilogue

The Prorok searched through the village of Rand, growing frustrated at his lack of success. *Where is he? I don't have much time!*

The Prorok had arrived at the barrier as it was falling apart. He had intended to help the new Valkyn reclaim his village, but on his way a set of visions assaulted him. When he awoke, the veins on his arms were glowing red as if they had been tattooed. His visions had lasted for days and it had taken him weeks to recover his strength to make the final part of the journey. No one made mention to him of the strange glowing patterns, really everyone sought to avoid conversation with what they perceived as a strange old coot, but he knew the meaning.

The visions were clear. He was dying, and somewhere on this frozen mountain was the boy that would take his place. The visions had shown him the boy's face. The Prorok was measuring the speed of the glow as it had spread up his arm. According to his observation, he only had a few months to live and to train the one who would be the new prophet of the Higher One. It wasn't the young Valkyn he had met in the woods, but someone even younger…

Made in the USA
Monee, IL
27 October 2021

80486626R00163